unspoken

Unspoken
Francine Rivers

TYNDALE HOUSE PUBLISHERS, INC.
WHEATON, ILLINOIS

Visit Tyndale's exciting Web site at www.tyndale.com

Check out the latest about Francine Rivers at www.francinerivers.com

"Seek and Find" section written by Peggy Lynch.

Edited by Kathryn S. Olson

Designed by Julie Chen

Library of Congress Cataloging-in-Publication Data

Rivers, Francine, date.
    Unspoken / Francine Rivers.
        p. cm. — (Lineage of grace)
    ISBN 0-8423-3598-6
        1. Bathsheba (Biblical figure)—Fiction. 2. Bible. O.T.—History of Biblical events—Fiction.
    3. Women in the Bible—Fiction. I. Title.

    PS3568.I83165 U49 2001
    813'.54—dc21   2001027224

Printed in the United States of America

06   05   04   03   02   01
9   8   7   6   5   4   3

For women who feel they've lost their reputation forever.
God can make beauty from ashes.

Rick, thank you for our prayer time and visit each morning.

It sets the tone for the rest of the day.

Thank you also for sharing your office,

building the fire on cold mornings, brewing the coffee,

and pausing in the hectic rush of running

your own business to let me brainstorm out loud about

whatever story happens to be running through my head.

Thank you, Jane Jordan Browne, for your constant encouragement

and friendship through the years. I've always

been able to depend on you.

Scott Mendel, thank you for your willingness

to respond (quickly!) to so many questions.

Thank you, Kathy Olson, for your fine editing and passion for Scripture.

I would like to also extend my thanks to the entire Tyndale staff

who have continued to follow Dr. Kenneth Taylor's mission

of glorifying the Lord—and who have encouraged me

as I strive to do likewise. I have felt blessed

over the years to be part of your team.

Thank you, Peggy Lynch, my dear friend and sister in Christ.

You have been a blessing to me from the day I met you.

You have always held up the lamp of God's Word.

Your life is a living testimony of faith.

The Lord has blessed me through all of you.

May those blessings return upon each of you a thousandfold.

DEAR READER,

This is the fourth of five novellas on the women in the lineage of Jesus Christ. These were Eastern women who lived in ancient times, and yet their stories apply to our lives and the difficult issues we face in our world today. They were on the edge. They had courage. They took risks. They did the unexpected. They lived daring lives, and sometimes they made mistakes—big mistakes. These women were not perfect, and yet God in His infinite mercy used them in His perfect plan to bring forth the Christ, the Savior of the world.

We live in desperate, troubled times when millions seek answers. These women point the way. The lessons we can learn from them are as applicable today as when they lived thousands of years ago.

Tamar is a woman of **hope.**
Rahab is a woman of **faith.**
Ruth is a woman of **love.**
Bathsheba is a woman who received **unlimited grace.**
Mary is a woman of **obedience.**

These are historical women who actually lived. Their stories, as I have told them, are based on biblical accounts. Although some of their actions may seem disagreeable to us in our century, we need to consider these women in the context of their own times.

This is a work of historical fiction. The outline of the story is provided by the Bible, and I have started with the facts provided for us there. Building on that foundation, I have created action, dialogue, internal motivations, and in some cases, additional characters that I feel are consistent with the biblical record. I have attempted to remain true to the scriptural message in all points, adding only what is necessary to aid in our understanding of that message.

At the end of each novella, we have included a brief study section. The ultimate authority on people of the Bible is the Bible itself. I encourage you to read it for greater understanding. And I pray that as you read the Bible, you will become aware of the continuity, the consistency, and the confirmation of God's plan for the ages—a plan that includes you.

Francine Rivers

THE powerful and mighty King Saul of Israel was jealous of a shepherd boy. The reason was simple: The Lord God had anointed this young man, David, as His chosen king. And more than that, David held the hearts of the people in his hands. When David spoke, people inclined their ear. When he danced, maidens swooned. When he sang, the hearts of men, women, and children rose in praise to God.

When David fled into the wilderness to escape Saul's murderous envy, hundreds of men followed him, camping with him in the caves of Adullam and En-gedi. Some were discontented men. Others were men hounded by Philistine raids. Some were men overtaxed by a king in whom they had lost confidence. And scattered among the honorable men, who longed for the days when God was Israel's supreme Commander, were men of violence and vengeance, men who simply loved shedding blood and grasping plunder.

War ripped the nation into factions as the king's jealousy mounted against his imagined enemy. But David was ever submissive to the king's authority. Refusing to wrest the crown from Saul by violent means, David was content to wait for God to act on his behalf.

Meanwhile, the company who gathered around David swelled steadily—from two hundred to four hundred to six hundred. Among them were thirty mighty men, an elite group of warriors of proven valor and loyalty. David's courage and integrity rallied them, and they held together like a family, fiercely intent upon protecting its own against all enemies, be they the king of Israel who had turned his back on God or the armies of the idol-infested nations surrounding them.

These valiant fighting men did not come alone to fight for David. They brought their wives and sons and daughters with them.

Traveling among the growing throng of David's followers was a little girl named Bathsheba. . . .

PERCHED on her grandfather's knee, Bathsheba tore off a piece of bread and offered it to him. Laughing, Ahithophel ate it from her hand. "She's becoming more like your mother every day, Eliam."

Her father watched her with a faint frown. "It's hard to believe she's growing up so fast. Eight years old already. It won't be long before I'll have to find a husband for her."

"A mighty man to protect a pretty young maiden."

She looked across the fire at the man who appeared, to her, like an angel from heaven. Tugging on her grandfather's tunic, stretching up, she whispered her heart's desire. "I want to marry David."

He laughed out loud and looked across at the handsome young man sitting across the fire. "David, here is another who has set you upon a pedestal." Heat flooded into her cheeks as the man she idolized looked back at her grandfather with embarrassed tolerance. Her grandfather kissed her cheek. "Forget David, Bathsheba. He has three wives already, my sweet." As he looked into her eyes, his amusement faded. His expression softened. "Better to be the only wife of a poor man than one woman among many in a king's harem."

"Come inside, Bathsheba!" her mother beckoned. Her grandfather lifted Bathsheba from his knee and set her firmly on her feet, sending her off with a light swat on her backside. When Bathsheba paused to look back at David, her mother caught her by the arm and yanked her inside the tent, flipping the flap down behind them. "It's time for bed." She followed Bathsheba and drew up the blanket as the girl lay down on her pallet. Kneeling, she leaned down and kissed Bathsheba. Troubled, she stroked the wisps of black hair back from Bathsheba's forehead. "Some dreams can only bring heartbreak."

"But I—"

Her mother put her fingertip over Bathsheba's lips. "Hush, child." She leaned back upon her heels and rose gracefully. "Go to sleep."

Bathsheba lay awake, listening to the men's voices rumbling quietly outside. Others had joined them. She recognized Joab's voice and that of his brother Abishai. Both were commanders of David's army, and they often came to talk war with her grandfather, who had earned David's respect for his shrewd tactical advice. He knew a great deal about the Philistines and Ammonites and their methods of battle. He also knew the land of Canaan as well as the lines in the palm of his own hand.

"Saul was in our hands, David," Joab said. "You should have killed him when you had the chance."

Joab's brother Abishai was quick to speak in agreement. "Yes, you need to kill Saul! God gave him to us in the Cave of the Wild Goats. I would have slit his throat for you."

"And I told you why I didn't want him killed," David said. "He is the man the Lord God anointed as king."

"He'll keep chasing you," Joab said. "He'll never stop until one of you is dead."

"It would be better for the nation if you took the crown from Saul now," another said. Bathsheba heard the rumble of agreement among several other men sitting at her father's campfire.

"Strike the shepherd and the sheep will scatter," Joab insisted.

"What am I to do with you sons of Zeruiah?" David said harshly, and she knew his impatience must be directed at Joab and Abishai. "How many times must I tell you I will not raise my hand against the Lord's anointed!"

She heard footsteps moving away.

"I don't understand him," Joab said in frustration. "Speak sense to him, Ahithophel!"

"What would David have gained by murdering the king while he had turned his back to relieve himself?" Her grandfather spoke calmly in the face of the younger men's hot tempers. "When Saul heard David call to him from the cave, he knew David could have killed him—yet David allowed him to walk away with only his pride injured.

Would a man who coveted his kingdom have done that? Of course not! Every man riding with Saul now knows David is in the right! And they know David was giving King Saul the chance to repent!"

"Repent! The fire in Saul's belly will be back soon enough, and we'll be on the run again. Should we spare a man who ordered the murder of eighty-five priests and their families at Nob?"

"Leave judgment to the Lord. David's course is a righteous one."

"You know as well as I that as long as there is breath in Saul's body, he will hunt David!"

"I know, too, that God will prevail, Joab. It will be by His efforts, not yours, that David will one day be king. The Lord is in command. Every day, more men join us. Why? Because they believe as we do: that God is with David wherever he goes. The Philistines, Ammonites, and Amalekites cannot defeat a man who has the Lord God of Israel as his shield."

"I want to see the crown on David's head!"

"So do we all, Joab. But let it happen in God's time and not before."

The men went on talking. Bathsheba's eyes were heavy with sleep. She dreamed of David dressed in royal robes, holding out his hand to her. Startled awake, she lay still, listening. Men were shouting in the distance. Probably another argument. She heard familiar voices outside. Rising to her knees, she peered between the stitches of the tent seam. David had returned and was sitting in the flickering firelight, talking with her father and grandfather.

"We'll join forces with the Philistines," David was saying. "When the fighting turns against Saul, we'll be in a position to turn the battle in his favor."

Her grandfather frowned in concentration. "How many do you plan to take?"

"All of them."

"Who will protect our women and children . . . ?"

Bathsheba gazed at David, her head full of dreams. She loved the way he tilted his head as he listened intently to what her grandfather had to say. She studied every line of his face.

Men shouted again. Her mother moaned softly, rolling over on her pallet. Bathsheba looked out again. David had his head turned toward the disturbance. A muscle in his jaw clenched. "These men are too much for me to manage!"

Her grandfather sat with his hands clasped between his knees. "They are a flock of sheep in need of a strong shepherd."

"Sometimes they behave more like a pack of wolves!" David shook his head and rose. "I guess I should do something." Sighing, he walked away.

"I don't understand him," her father said, tossing a rock into the darkness. "Why is he always coming to Saul's rescue even when it could mean his own death?"

"Have you forgotten that Saul's son Jonathan is David's closest friend? And David's first wife is Saul's daughter."

"Jonathan has chosen sides, Abba, and Michal is defiled. Saul gave her to another man. David lives in hope that everything will change back to the way it was before Saul went mad with jealousy. It will never happen."

Her grandfather poked the fire. "Joab's advice is shrewd. Saul's death would put an end to this war and place David on the throne. But there would be no blessing for David if he kills the Lord's anointed. Ah, my son, David lives to please God. His passion is for the Lord." He looked up, his face aglow. "If every man among us had the heart David has, what a kingdom God would build for us!" Tossing the stick into the fire, he rose. "Come, let's stand with our friend and hear what the Lord has given him to say this time."

Bathsheba knew David wouldn't shout orders at the fighting men, nor interfere with their arguments. Instead he would simply sit near them and sing. She waited, and after a little while, she could hear the sound of his harp amidst the shouting—a soothing melody played quietly against angry, discordant voices. Already the angry voices were dying down. Pulling at the seams, Bathsheba tried to see more from within the narrow view of her father's tent. Her grandfather always said that God gave David's words and music the power to lift hearts and minds from petty differences to God's majesty and the blessings He had poured upon His chosen people. She had heard David play and sing many times before, and she never tired of it.

Her mother was asleep. What harm if she snuck out and crept close enough to watch and listen? She slipped through the flaps and hastened toward the gathering, staying at the edge of firelight. Hunkering down, arms wrapped around her knees, she sat and listened. Her young heart trembled at the sight of David, his handsome face bronzed in the firelight. No one in the entire world could be as perfect as David, her beloved.

"O Lord, our Lord, the majesty of your name fills the earth!" His voice rang out in the night air. His words grew indistinct when he turned away. So she rose and crept closer. One by one, men sat and reclined, gazing up at David as they listened, captivated as he worshiped God more openly than any priest. David stopped in the midst of his men and lifted his head, singing a wordless melody that made Bathsheba's heart ache. Then lyrics came again to him.

"When I look at the night sky and see the work of your fingers—the moon and the stars you have set in place— what are mortals that you should think of us, mere humans that you should care for us?"

Everyone was silent now, waiting as David bowed his head and plucked the strings of his harp. The sound and words pierced her so deeply that Bathsheba felt he was plucking the strings of her heart. "For you made us only a little lower than God, and you crowned us with glory and honor. You put us in charge of everything you made, giving us authority over all things—the sheep and the cattle and all the wild animals, the birds in the sky, the fish in the sea, and everything that swims the ocean currents." David shook his head in wonder and looked up at the stars again, his face rapt. "O Lord, our Lord, the majesty of your name fills the earth!" He played a few more chords on his harp and then lifted his hand slowly above his head, offering his words of praise to the God of all creation.

And the camp was quiet—so quiet, Bathsheba could hear her own heartbeat.

"Sing another psalm, David," her grandfather, Ahithophel, said.

Others joined in his appeal. "Sing to us of the Lord!"

Bathsheba rose and crept in among the gathering, slipping in next to her doting grandfather, seeking his warmth. "What are you doing up?" he whispered gruffly and put his arm around her, snuggling her close.

"I had to hear, and I was getting cold." Shivering, she looked up at him pleadingly. "Please, Grandpapa, just for a little while . . . ?"

"You know I can't say no to you." He pulled his cloak around her. "One song."

David sang another psalm, one she had heard many times before. His handsome face glowed in the firelight, and his words poured forth upon her thirsty soul. Unlike so many hearts around her, David's heart wasn't turned toward war. He longed for peace. He appealed to God for help and mercy and deliverance from his enemies. What would it be like to live without fear of a pursuing king, of Philistines and Ammonites, of the raiding Amalekites? She looked at her father and saw his eyes were moist as he leaned forward, listening intently. How many times had she heard her papa say God would uphold their cause? God would hide them in the cleft of the rocks and inside the caves of En-gedi and Adullam. God would sustain them with food and water. God would give them victory against every enemy. Why? Because they were with David, and David did nothing without inquiring of the Lord. David prayed his songs, and God listened.

David walked a few steps and stood for a moment with his head bowed. His eyes were closed. She watched his hands move gently over the strings, strumming softly and making her heart ache. He raised his head and looked from face to face. Would he look at her? Would he notice her sitting between her father and grandfather?

"The Lord is my shepherd; I have everything I need. . . ."

When David's gaze fixed upon her, her heart leaped into her throat. She held her breath, staring back at him, but his gaze moved on, touching each man there as though every one was equally precious to him. She felt crushed beneath the pressure of her love for him, and dejected that he hardly noticed her among his throng of devoted followers.

You are my shepherd, David. You make me want something I can't even name. You lead us through the wilderness, but I'm not afraid, because you are with us. And I would do anything for you. . . .

Someone gripped her shoulder tightly, startling her. "Bathsheba!" her mother whispered angrily.

"So you've been caught again," her grandfather whispered, unfurling his cloak from around her back and shoulders. Scowling, her mother scooped her up and carried her away, setting her on her feet when they were halfway back to the family tent. "You're lucky I don't take a rod to you!" Lowering her eyes, Bathsheba followed her mother through the darkness. Her mother swished the tent flap back. "Get inside!" Once past the opening, her mother gave her a swat on her behind. "Since I can't trust you to stay where you

belong, you'll sleep beside me until your father returns."
Her mother drew her close. "You know better than to
disobey."

Bathsheba sniffled. "I'm sorry, Mama. It's just that I love
him."

Her mother sighed. "I know you do. We all love David."

"Not like I do. I'm going to marry him someday."

Her mother's arms tightened around her. "Oh, my sweet
one. Every girl among us wishes for the same thing. You
must listen to me, Bathsheba. What you hope for is impossi-
ble. It's the idle dream of a child."

"Why?"

"Because David is too far above you."

Her throat tightened. "He was a shepherd."

"He still is a shepherd, but not in the way you mean. You
must understand. David is destined to be *king,* and as such,
he will marry the daughters of kings. You're only the
daughter of one of his soldiers."

"Abba is a warrior, one of David's *best* warriors, and one
of his *closest* friends. And Grandpapa . . ."

"*Hush!* Remember, David is still married to Saul's daughter Michal, even though Saul gave her to someone else. And
David is also married to Ahinoam and Abigail."

"Abigail isn't the daughter of a king," Bathsheba said
stubbornly.

"No, but Abigail kept David from committing a great sin.
He was grateful for her wisdom. And she is very beautiful."

"Do you think I'll be beautiful someday, beautiful
enough—"

"Someday, you'll be very beautiful, and wiser than you

are right now, I hope. At the very least, wise enough to understand that some things are not meant to be. Your father will find a good husband for you, and you'll forget you ever thought yourself in love with David."

Never! Never, never, never! Bathsheba blinked back tears and turned her head away.

"When you grow up, my love, you will understand the wisdom of worshiping God and not a man."

Bathsheba lay still until she heard the sound of her mother's deepened breathing. Then she eased out of her arms and crawled to the other side of the tent to peer into the night once more. Her father and grandfather had returned to the fire, and David had joined them once again. They spoke quietly of battle plans. Bathsheba closed her eyes and listened to the sound of David's voice. Content, she fell asleep.

✦   ✦   ✦

When she awakened the next morning, Bathsheba found herself on her pallet, under her blanket. Her father snored beside her mother. Bathsheba rose quietly and left the tent. David would be up by now. He was always up before everyone else, and he always went off by himself to pray. She had seen him several times coming back from the stream, so she hurried toward it now. Her heartbeat quickened when she spotted David kneeling by a rippling pool, washing his face, arms, and hands. Her father and grandfather always did the same thing before they prayed.

Her footfall caused a soft cascade of pebbles to spill down the slope. David turned sharply, eyes intent, hand on the hilt of his sword. When he saw her, he relaxed.

"You're up early, Bathsheba. Aren't you a little far from camp?"

Her heart hammered as she came closer. "I came to get water."

"Then you have a problem, little one."

"What problem?"

He smiled. "You have no jug."

Heat surged into her cheeks. When he started to turn away, she spoke quickly before she lost all her courage. "Could we talk awhile, David? I came all this way to see you."

He turned and looked at her. "You shouldn't be so far from camp. It's dangerous. Go on back to your tent where you belong."

"But—"

"You know your mother wouldn't be happy you strayed so far. I don't think she'd be pleased if she had to come searching for you a second time."

Crushed by his reprimand, Bathsheba bolted up the slope, ducked behind some rocks, and sat down heavily. Trembling, she put her cold palms against her burning cheeks. Then she took a breath and peered out from her hiding place. David was still standing by the stream, his hands now on his hips. "Go home before you're missed! And don't leave the camp again!"

Sucking in a sob, Bathsheba clambered up and ran all the rest of the way back to her father's tent, thankful no one was awake to see her tears—or ask the cause of them.

✦   ✦   ✦

Word came that the Philistines were going out against Saul. Bathsheba's grandfather and father laid out their armor and weapons. Bathsheba helped her mother prepare parched grain and raisin cakes for them to take with them. Her mother was silent, as she always was before the men left. So, too, was Bathsheba as she listened to them talk.

"We go tomorrow and join the ranks of Philistines," her grandfather said. Bathsheba remembered the plan she had overheard David talking about. His men would only be pretending to help the Philistines. Really, they were waiting for a chance to help King Saul defeat this enemy army.

"Surely they'll suspect David's offer as pretense," her father said tightly. "It's only through God's mercy that we haven't been caught raiding the Geshurite and Amalekite villages these past years."

"We've timed our raids carefully and left no survivors."

"Rumors spread . . ."

"David wants to be in a position to help Saul. If the Philistines reject our offer of aid, there'll be nothing we can do."

"Saul's fate is in God's hands already, and I don't like leaving our women and children on their own."

As the sun rose the next morning, Bathsheba watched her father and grandfather leave camp with David. As soon as they were out of sight, her mother went inside the tent and wept. She was quickly herself again. She sat in the shade of the tent carding wool and sent Bathsheba off with the sheep.

The day after the men left, Bathsheba was bringing water up from the stream when she heard yelling and screaming. Dropping the skin, she ran up the bank. Amalekite raiders were charging into the camp while women fled in a dozen directions, grabbing up their children as they ran. Defense-less, they were quickly rounded up like a scattered flock.

When Bathsheba saw a man knock her mother to the ground and try to tie a rope around her flailing hands, she shrieked and ran at him in a fury. Jumping on his back, she clawed his forehead and yanked his hair. "Let her go! Let my mother go!"

With an angry shout, the man caught hold of her hair and hurled her over his shoulder. She hit the ground hard. Gasping for breath, she made it to her hands and knees, but someone looped a rope around her neck. Rolling over, she grabbed it and kicked the man. He uttered a harsh groan and bent over, his face going white while one of his company called out a laughing insult. "Is that little flea too much to handle?"

Enraged, the Amalekite gave the rope a hard yank. As she choked, he dragged her up by her arm and shook her violently. "Fight me and I'll drag you to your death!" He sent her flying into the line of women and children.

Sobbing, her mother quickly loosened the rope and clasped her close. "Bathsheba! Oh, Bathsheba!"

Bathsheba coughed violently and wretched and dragged in a full, painful breath. "David will—" Her mother clapped a hand over her mouth and shushed her. She'd never seen terror in her mother's face before this day.

The Amalekite guard turned on her. *"No talking!"*

The women and older children were tied and led away. Younger children were carried. The band of raiders and captives walked for hours, the midday heat bearing down hard upon the women and children, who were given only enough water to keep them going. They stopped as the sun was setting. Most of the women collapsed, too tired even to whimper. Each captive was given a handful of parched grain.

Bathsheba ate ravenously, but her stomach still ached with hunger. Her neck was bruised and burned from the rope. Her throat hurt from the hard yank she'd received early that day. Her feet were raw from walking across dusty, rocky ground. Her body ached all over. When she began to cry, her mother pulled her close and shared her body warmth as the moon and stars appeared and the temperature plummeted.

"I'm afraid, Mother." Bathsheba cried softly.

Her mother stroked her hair back from her sunburned face. "It does no good to cry. We need to save our strength for whatever lies ahead."

"David will come looking for us, won't he?"

"We will pray that he and your father return quickly." She held Bathsheba tighter. Bathsheba felt her mother trembling and asked no more questions. "Pray, my daughter. Pray hard."

And Bathsheba did. *David, oh, David, come and find us. Come and save us!*

The Amalekites kept the women on the move, hastening them toward a future of slavery, prostitution, and death. Exhausted, the women and children collapsed each night, too bone weary to cause their captors trouble of any kind. After the first two nights, they were left unbound while the men sat around the campfire, drinking and laughing. No guards watched over them. There was no need after so many miles of travel.

When the sun rose and set on the third day, hope waned.

✦   ✦   ✦

Bathsheba awakened abruptly to the sound of battle cries. The air around her reverberated with shouts and screams. Confused and terrified, she tried to rise, but her mother grabbed her. "Stay down!" She pulled her back and down as a nearby Amalekite grabbed for his sword. He fell back with a scream, his arm severed, and then his head as well. Horrified, Bathsheba looked up at the attacking warrior who jumped across the lifeless body. Her father's friend Uriah! Shouting his battle cry, he charged on. If Uriah was here, surely her father was also, and her grandfather.

"Abba!" Bathsheba screamed. *"Abba!"*

The Amalekites fell back and tried to run, but they were cut down without mercy by avenging fathers, husbands, and brothers. Bathsheba saw Ittai the Gittite hack, from shoulder to sternum, the guard who had choked her. The roar of battle was terrifying. Israelites cried out in wrath; Amalekites screamed in terror. The clash of swords and thunder of men's feet were all around her as she cowered against her mother.

And then it was over. As quickly as it had started, it ended, and the silence was a shock. The bloodied bodies of the Amalekite raiders lay sprawled around the camp, while the men left standing were no less terrifying in their stained garments, their hands and arms and weapons splashed with red.

Bathsheba heard David call out, "Ahinoam! Abigail!"

Other men cried out names as well, searching for their wives and children.

"Here! I'm here!" women cried back. All was still in confusion.

"Eliam!" Her mother let go of her and ran into her father's arms, sobbing against his chest.

"Bathsheba," he said raggedly and held out his arm, but she couldn't move at the sight of him covered in blood. His eyes were so fierce he looked like a stranger. "Come, Daughter," he said more gently, still breathing hard. "Come to me. I won't hurt you." Trembling violently, she looked away and saw the carnage around her.

Her grandfather was there suddenly, catching her up in his arms, holding her close. "You are safe, my little flower." Over his shoulder, Bathsheba saw David speaking with Ahinoam and Abigail. She lost sight of him again when her grandfather put her back on her feet, his hand firmly upon her shoulder, keeping her against his side. "War is always worse for the children," he said gruffly.

"I didn't think you'd be able to find us," her mother said, her arms still around Bathsheba's father. "Oh, Eliam, you would've been proud of your daughter." She told him about everything from the day the Amalekites had raided the camp.

Bathsheba closed her eyes, but even then she couldn't block out the picture of the slaughter around her. She was cold and couldn't stop shaking. She understood now why her mother cried every time her father left camp with David.

"The Philistines turned us away," her father said. "If they

hadn't, we might not have been able to track you so quickly."

Her mother frowned. "Saul?"

"He's outnumbered."

"What will David do?"

"The only thing he can do. Nothing."

On the way back to camp, some of the men argued over the share of spoils they'd taken from the Amalekite camp. They were not willing to share with those who had been too tired to cross the river. David commanded that the spoils be divided equally among all the men, with gifts to be sent to the elders of Israel's cities.

And so it was done, but not without grumbling.

✦ ✦ ✦

An Amalekite came into David's camp, bearing news of Israel's defeat. Bathsheba was listening when he told David that Saul and his son Jonathan had been killed by the Philistines at Mount Gilboa. Their bodies were hanging on the wall of Beth-shan, while Saul's weapons had been placed in the temple of Ashtoreth. When the messenger stepped forward and stretched out his arms, murmurs issued from David's men, who stood by, watching. The Amalekite smiled broadly, triumphant, as he offered David Saul's crown.

David looked at it and began to shake with rage. Bathsheba wondered why he was so angry. David took the proffered crown. "How do you know that Saul and Jonathan are dead?" he demanded.

The man's eyes flickered. Perhaps the Amalekite sensed something ominous in David's tone. "I happened to be on

Mount Gilboa," he answered. "I saw Saul there leaning on his spear with the enemy chariots closing in on him. When he turned and saw me, he cried out for me to come to him. 'How can I help?' I asked him. And he said to me, 'Who are you?' I replied, 'I am an Amalekite.' Then he begged me, 'Come over here and put me out of my misery, for I am in terrible pain and want to die.' So I killed him," the Amalekite told David, "for I knew he couldn't live. Then I took his crown and one of his bracelets so I could bring them to you, my lord."

Even from her vantage point, Bathsheba could see the blood drain from David's face. "Were you not afraid to kill the Lord's anointed one?" he cried. As the man shifted his weight, David said to one of his men, "Kill him!" So the man thrust his sword into the Amalekite.

"You die self-condemned!" David spoke into the impaled man's face. "For you yourself confessed that you killed the Lord's anointed one." He yanked the sword from the Amalekite and watched him crumple to the ground.

David must have felt the eyes of all upon him, for he looked around at the silent men, women, and children staring at what he'd done. Bathsheba longed to understand, to share his grief. His emotions burst forth and he cried out, "Your pride and joy, O Israel, lies dead on the hills! How the mighty heroes have fallen! O King Saul!" He sobbed, dropping the sword and holding his head. "Oh, Jonathan! Jonathan, my brother!"

David's grief infected the entire camp as everyone mourned the death of King Saul and David's best friend, Jonathan. David sang songs of tribute to them, reminding the people of the good days when Saul had loved the Lord and served Him.

And when the period of mourning came to an end, David obeyed the Lord and moved his army to Hebron.

✦   ✦   ✦

It was at Hebron that Bathsheba watched David marry Maacah. Through the years she watched him marry Haggith, Abital, and Eglah, and with each wedding, she heard he made important alliances. He needed allies, for despite Saul's death, the house of Saul continued to wage war upon David. "He has an eye for beautiful women," she heard her grandfather say. Amnon was born to Ahinoam, Kileab to Abigail, Absalom to Maacah.

Messengers came from Abner, commander of the army of Saul's son Ishbosheth, proposing an alliance. Bathsheba's grandfather advised David to be cautious and test Abner's sincerity and strength. So David sent word that he would not agree to anything unless his first wife, Saul's daughter Michal, was returned to him.

"He must love her very much," Bathsheba said. She still could not look at David without feeling a quickening inside her, but she was more clear-sighted now that she was almost grown than she had been as a small child. She no longer clung so tenaciously to her fantasies of marrying the man of her dreams.

Her mother shook her head. "Love has nothing to do with it. What rightfully belonged to David must be restored. He will take Michal into his house, but she will never have children."

"All of his other wives have had children. She will also."

"Your grandfather will advise against it. She's been defiled by adultery. King Saul gave her to another man years ago, when you were just a baby. Besides that, should David beget a child by her and build the house of Saul? May it never be! David will listen to your grandfather. He will provide for Michal and protect her, but he will never touch her again."

Bathsheba felt pity for Michal. "It would have been kinder to leave her with the other man." And David would have one less wife, one less beautiful woman in his household.

"Perhaps," her mother said quietly. "I heard that the man followed her for miles, weeping and wailing. Abner had to order him away. But David is a king, Bathsheba. He is not an ordinary man."

"No one could ever have called David ordinary, even before he was king."

Her mother looked at her solemnly. Bathsheba smiled. "Don't worry, Mother. I know I am only the daughter of a humble warrior." Something flickered in her mother's eyes. Bathsheba turned away. "If David will never have children with Michal, why is it so important she be returned to him?"

"He must prove himself strong. A king who cannot keep possession of the women who belong to him cannot hold a kingdom together."

Bathsheba knew David was strong enough. What strength he lacked God would provide. She looked toward his tent. "Do you think she loves him?"

"She did once. She even saved his life. But that was years ago."

"I don't think he loves her anymore. I don't think he's ever given his heart to any woman, not completely."

"Oh, my dear." Her mother sighed heavily. "It is wiser for a woman to fall in love with a poor man who can afford only one wife." Bathsheba's throat closed hot, and she blinked back tears as her mother rose and came to her, turning her around and tipping her chin up. "You became a woman a month ago. I spoke with your father and he says someone has already spoken to him regarding you."

Bathsheba's heart pounded with trepidation. "Who?"

Her mother smiled. "A good man. A strong one."

"Who is it?"

"I won't say until it's settled, but if it comes to be, you will have a husband you can respect."

"Respect, but not love."

"In time, love, too. If you allow it."

+ + +

Bathsheba's father and grandfather accepted the bride-price from Uriah the Hittite, and all, in their minds, was settled. Her mother, in an effort to encourage her, explained their many reasons for choosing him. Uriah had saved her father once in battle; Uriah was counted among David's thirty mighty men; Uriah had proven himself valorous and dependable in hard times. Ahithophel had seen Uriah charge into the hottest battle without fear in order to defend David. He was admired and respected by all, and a friend of the king. Such a man would be able to protect her and provide for her and the children she would give him.

"He's a courageous man, Bathsheba, and he's loyal. He's been wise with his possessions. Unlike others, Uriah hasn't squandered the spoils he gathered in battles against the Philistines and Amalekites."

"But he's so much older than I am!"

Her mother looked her in the eyes. "He's a year younger than David."

Bathsheba sat heavily, covered her face, and wept in defeat. She was a woman—albeit a young one—and had no say in the matter. The decision regarding whom she would marry had never been hers, and she'd always known in her heart that David was as far beyond her reach as a star in the heavens. She was nothing but a foolish, earthbound child clinging to her dreams, but, oh, how it hurt to have them wrenched from her. Years ago, David had been chosen by God and anointed by Samuel to one day be king of Israel. Who was she to think she was worthy to be his wife—or even his concubine? What wretched misery to fall in love with a man who was a king!

"If only he'd been an ordinary shepherd . . ."

Her mother stamped her foot. "*Enough of this foolishness! Enough dreaming!* I will not have my daughter act like a self-ish child! You should thank God David is more than a shepherd! Where would our people be if he'd never left the pastures and his father's flocks? Even if you were the daughter of a king and worthy to marry him, what then? Could you bear to watch him take more wives and concubines? A king must build a strong house and preserve the kingdom. You would have to put your own desires aside for the sake of a nation that depends upon him."

Her mother grasped her shoulders tightly. "Your father has chosen a fine man for you. Uriah is good and decent, and you will be his *only* wife. David has never so much as glanced at you, Bathsheba, but Uriah looks upon you as though you were a pearl of great price. You will be his most prized possession."

Bathsheba felt ashamed. "I have nothing against Uriah, Mother. It's only that I . . ." Tears streamed down her face. She knew it was useless to say another word. Could she change the inevitable?

Her mother let go of her abruptly and moved away. "No one expects you to love Uriah right away, Bathsheba. In time, you will—if you give him a chance." She turned and looked at her. "But for now, you *will* show Uriah the respect and obedience he deserves as your husband. If you don't, I will take a whip to you myself!"

Bathsheba raised her chin. "I will marry Uriah, Mother, and I will show him the respect and obedience he deserves. But love cannot be commanded."

For as long as she could remember, her heart and soul had belonged to David. And she knew that would never change, no matter what others demanded of her.

✦　✦　✦

Bathsheba never expected David to come to her wedding. When she saw him through the colored gauze of her veils, she almost wept at the pain, knowing he had come not to see her become a wife, but to honor his friend, her husband.

Uriah was dressed like a king for the ceremony. Even then, her husband paled in comparison to her true sovereign lord, who wore a simple tunic and leather girdle. David outshone every man at the ceremony! And even though he placed a groom's crown upon Uriah's head, there could be no comparison between them. There was a nobility about David that proclaimed his place among men. No one was more handsome and graceful. No one could surpass his gifts of music and dance. No one held a position of greater power, nor had a more humble, tender heart. David asked for no special treatment, but everyone deferred to him out of love and respect. God had blessed David in every way.

The wedding feast proceeded with Bathsheba in a haze. She was relieved when Uriah left her side to greet David. They laughed together and shared a goblet of wine while she sat on the dais and watched. It was David who drew her husband back to her side. It was David who took up a pitcher and replenished Uriah's cup and then filled hers. She brushed his fingers with her own as she took the goblet, sensing his surprise. Did he think she was bold?

"May the Lord bless your house with many children, Uriah," David said grandly, and in a voice loud enough to carry. He raised his cup high. Bathsheba raised her eyes and looked into his, and for an infinitesimal moment, she felt something change between them. Heat spread over her skin. "And," he continued, "may all your sons and daughters look like your wife and not like you." He looked into her eyes as he sipped, his own strangely dark and perplexed.

The men around them laughed, Uriah loudest of all. David blinked and then laughed as well, slapping Uriah on the back and saying something to him that was lost in the din surrounding her. Uriah nodded and looked at her proudly, his eyes glowing. David's eyes met hers again, and her stomach fluttered strangely. The moment was both enticing and terrifying. When Uriah looked at her, she felt nothing. But David's look made her cheeks burn and her heart hammer. She lowered her eyes, startled by the powerful feelings surging inside her. She glanced around cautiously, wondering if anyone had noticed the effect David had upon her. She was trembling. Afraid, she looked at her mother, but she was dancing and laughing with the other women, and her father and grandfather were drinking with the men.

Turning her head shyly, she encountered David's stare. It shook her deeply, for she instinctively understood its meaning. Exultation was overwhelmed by despair.

Why does he look at me as a woman now, when it's too late? Why couldn't he have noticed me a new moon ago?

Uriah came and sat with her upon the dais. He took her hand and kissed it, his eyes bright from admiration and too much wine. "I am blessed among men," he said thickly. "There is not a man here, including our king, who does not envy me such a beautiful young wife."

She smiled back tremulously, embarrassed by his impassioned compliment.

The wedding feast wore on until she was emotionally exhausted. She forced a smile until her cheeks ached. She pretended to be happy, pretended she wasn't drowning in a sea of sorrow. Twice more, David looked at her. And twice, she looked back at him, fighting against the tears. He always looked away quickly, as though caught doing something that made him ashamed. And that made her suffer all the more.

Oh, David, David, what a wretched woman I am. I love you! I'll always love you the same way I have since I was a little girl. Do you remember how I followed you to the stream of En-gedi and watched you pray? I was just a child, but love caught me and held me tight in its grip. Nothing can kill it. And now I'm married to a man I can never love because I gave my heart to you years ago!

When David rose and left, she was almost relieved.

✦   ✦   ✦

Uriah was a man hardened by years of fighting the Philistines, Amalekites, and King Saul, but Bathsheba found him surprisingly kind as well. "I don't know anything about women, Bathsheba. I've spent my entire life training for battle and fighting alongside David. And that won't change. My allegiance will always be to David first, for he is God's anointed. But I promise I will take care of you. And if anything should happen to me, you will have enough so that you will always have a roof over your head and food to eat." His hands were callused from using his sword, and he shook when he touched her. "Please don't cry."

She wept because Uriah deserved to be loved, and she had no love left to give him.

✦   ✦   ✦

As the months passed, Bathsheba gave up her dreams and fulfilled her duties to her husband. She carried water from the well. She washed, cooked, cleaned, and carded wool. She wove cloth and made garments for her husband. She did everything she knew how to make her husband's life comfortable and pleasant. And though she did come to respect him, she could not *will* herself to fall in love with him.

Uriah spent most of his time with the other mighty men, training David's army, sparring, talking, and planning late into the night. Sometimes he brought soldiers home with him. He told her to keep her face covered so the men wouldn't stare when she served them. He told her to cover her face when she left the house. "There are rough men among David's army, men who have no respect for women."

"I've known such men all my life, Uriah. No one has ever bothered me before."

"Before, you were a child, Bathsheba. Now, you're a beautiful young woman. And you are my wife. Obey me." He tipped her chin and looked into her eyes. "It is always wise to avoid trouble."

Uriah and the other mighty men talked freely while they ate and drank, and by listening, Bathsheba learned much of what was going on in Canaan. She knew within hours that Joab, David's commander, had murdered a man in vengeance. She heard how furious David was, and how he mourned the murdered man. She was among the people when David condemned Joab's actions as evil. She was afraid for David because Joab was a powerful man, and a proud one as well. Why would David retain Joab as commander over his army?

Nothing came of David's reproach, but soon more news changed the course of Bathsheba's life. Ishbosheth, son of

Saul and heir to the throne of Israel, was murdered. The men who came with news of the assassination thought David would be pleased to have his rival removed. Now the way was clear for David to assume his rightful place as king over all of Israel! They even brought the head of Ishbosheth with them to prove their foul deed. Rather than rewarding them, though, David had them executed. He ordered their hands and feet cut off and their bodies hung up beside the pool of Hebron.

Many of the men Uriah brought home were violent, more comfortable in war than in peace. Her house was constantly filled with stories of intrigue surrounding David. Why was there such cruelty in the world? And if David was ever crowned king over all Israel, would there be those who would try to assassinate him, just like Saul and Ishbosheth before him?

Often, she would remember her mother's words: *"The life of a king is never easy. . . . Better to love a poor man . . ."* It was not easy to be the wife of a warrior either, for she never knew from one battle to the next whether she would be left a childless widow. "I live in fear every day, wondering if I'll lose your father," her mother admitted when they talked at the community well.

What would happen to Uriah's household if he died now? Bathsheba had no children, but not for want of trying. She wondered if her husband was disappointed in her, but if he was, she saw no sign of it. Two years had come and gone since their wedding feast, and he still treated her with kindness.

All the tribes of Israel gathered at Hebron, appearing

before David and declaring that he was God's anointed. "We are all members of your family," the high priest said to him before the people. "For a long time, even while Saul was our king, you were the one who really led Israel. And the Lord has told you, 'You will be the shepherd of My people Israel. You will be their leader.'"

Bathsheba's heart swelled with pride as she stood among the crowd and watched David make a covenant with the people and be anointed king of Israel. He was only thirty years old, and yet the elders of all the tribes bowed down before him. And Uriah stood nearby, one of David's bodyguards and closest friends, raising his hands to heaven and shouting in exultation.

And then David went to war again, Uriah at his side.

+   +   +

Bathsheba waited with the other wives to receive word about the battle for Zion, and when it came, she cried out in joy with all the rest.

"They've taken Jerusalem!"

But neither David nor Uriah came home to Hebron. Instead, they sent a contingent of warriors to bring the families to the newly conquered mountain stronghold. Building commenced all around the City of David, strengthening Zion for defense. Walls were built. Hiram, king of Tyre, sent cedar trees and carpenters and stonemasons to build a house for David. And Uriah chose a stone house near the site of the king's palace.

Still, peace was elusive. The Philistines gathered against David, spreading out across the valley of Rephaim. And once again, Uriah was called away to war. Bathsheba cried this time, for she had come to care very deeply for him.

"Don't fear for me. The Lord is on our side!" was his parting exhortation. His words were of no comfort to her. She had no son to carry on Uriah's name or to take care of her when she was old.

Word returned that the Philistines were defeated at Baal-perazim. When Uriah came home with an idol, Bathsheba protested. It was the first time in their marriage that she dared argue with her husband. But she knew how detestable idols were to the Lord God. "Would it please God to know you have set that loathsome thing in our house?"

"It means nothing. Everyone carried something from the field of battle. It's a memento of our triumph. Nothing more."

"David wouldn't bring something unclean into *his* house. You should've destroyed it!"

His eyes darkened with the fierce pride of a victorious warrior. "Don't tell me what I should've done! What are you afraid of, woman? It's nothing but clay. Did it save the man who owned it?"

"It's a thing of evil, Uriah!"

He tossed his armor aside and glared at her. "Do you think I don't know there is only one God? It's the Lord who has given David victory on every side! And you'll leave that idol where it stands as a reminder of a battle *I* fought alongside my king, the battle *I* helped win!"

Ashamed of having spoken out so forcefully, Bathsheba said no more.

The Philistines regrouped, and again, Uriah was called

away to war. The Philistines were like a plague that lingered. The Lord gave David victory again, and the Philistines were struck down from Geba as far as Gezer. But Bathsheba knew it would never be over. Men's hearts seemed bent upon war. Uriah's most of all.

Uriah didn't return home. It was her mother who told her that her father and Uriah had gone with David to Baalah of Judah to bring the Ark of God back to Jerusalem. Bathsheba ran down the road with the other women and wept in relief when they returned. Her joy was quickly dampened by their manner, for the Ark was not with them. David looked neither to the right nor to the left as he rode by on his mule. His face was dust-covered and tense. When she spotted Uriah, Bathsheba kept pace with him along the road. An air of defeat hung over them. David gave orders to disperse the men and went up to his house and his wives.

Uriah came to her then. She'd never seen him so tired. She lowered her shawl from her face and searched his eyes.

"What's happened, Uriah?"

"David's afraid to bring the Ark to Jerusalem."

"David's never been afraid of anything."

His jaw clenched. He took her arm and turned her toward home. "He's afraid of God. We all are. Uzzah, the priest's son, is dead. He laid hands on the Ark when the oxen stumbled, and the Lord struck him down. I've never seen a man die so fast." His hand loosened. "He went down as though hit by a thunderbolt."

"Where's the Ark now?"

"At the house of Obed-edom of Gath, where it will stay until the Lord tells David otherwise."

With Uriah home, the house became a gathering place again as soldiers came often to pass time with Bathsheba's husband. Sometimes they lingered late into the night. They could talk of little else but the continuing reports of how God was blessing the household of Obed-edom. After three months of such tidings, David summoned his mighty men and went down for the Ark. Uriah was among them.

+ + +

From a great distance came the sound of trumpets and shouting, announcing the return of David's mighty men. Women swept out into the street and ran to meet the procession. Jubilant, Bathsheba raced down the mountain road with them. Sunlight shone off the Ark and she thrilled at the sight of it. Each time the men who were carrying it had gone six steps, they stopped and waited so David could sacrifice an ox and a fattened calf. Trumpets sounded. And David danced with all his might. Men, women, and children sang and wept. Stripping off his outer garment, David continued leading the procession, dancing in his tunic. The people caught his zeal for the Lord. Men sang out praise after praise to God as women joined David in dancing.

The hard years were over at last. God had protected David and given him victory on every side! God had made him king over all Israel! The nations could not stand against him because God was on his side! The Lord had strength-ened him and built an army of mighty men around him, and now the Ark would rest upon the mountain where Abra-ham had once been ready to sacrifice his only son, Isaac, to God!

Bathsheba's racing blood sang with joy. She could not

stand still and watch. If she didn't cry out in praise and dance, she would go mad. Laughing and weeping, she tore away her shawl, lifting it high like a canopy over her head as she twirled, dipped, twisted, and was caught up in the ecstasy of the moment.

Peace would reign at last! No enemy could defeat them.

+   +   +

Yet, crouched at the door was a greater enemy than those who camped around Israel. And a greater battle was coming—one that could tear a nation to pieces. The battle would not take place in the mountains, valleys, or plains of Israel. It would take place in the wilderness of the human heart.

"HANUN did *what?*"

David leaned forward, scarcely able to believe the news he was hearing. He'd sent ambassadors to show respect for Nahash, the old king who'd allowed his father and mother to live among the Ammonites during the years King Saul had pursued him. He'd intended to make clear to Hanun, Nahash's son, that he had no intentions of invading. Yet now, he learned that his ambassadors had been insulted. Far worse, they'd been humiliated!

The dust-covered, sweating young messenger stepped closer and repeated his news in an embarrassed whisper. "King Hanun accused your ambassadors of being spies, Sire!" He grimaced as he rasped, "He had half their beards shaved off and their tunics cut to their buttocks. While his entire court laughed, he ordered them out of his palace!"

David shot to his feet. The men clustered in small groups around the court fell silent an instant before the room buzzed with whispered questions and speculations.

Joab had watched the exchange between David and the messenger with narrowed eyes, while Ahithophel and Eliam left their companions and strode across the room.

"Quiet!" Ahithophel shouted above the din. "The king speaks!"

David wished he hadn't shown his anger. He should have left the room with the messenger and heard the news in private. Then he could have heard everything and thought over what course he would take before the men knew what had happened. Joab's face was rigid. David knew he was ready to go to war, hungry for battle. Looking around the court, David saw they all were. Often he despaired at being around such violent men. Yet, what right had he to grumble to God, when his own blood was hot and crying out for revenge against Hanun?

The fool! Did he think he could insult Israel with impunity? Did he think there would be no repercussions? David would not ignore what had been done to his men. He couldn't afford to ignore Hanun's foolishness and risk losing the respect of his men. Worse, the nations around them would hear of any leniency shown and take it for weakness instead. If David didn't act soon, the Ammonites would think Israel was ripe for invasion. He didn't need to ask Ahithophel for advice. He knew what he had to do: teach this arrogant Ammonite king a lesson so that no one else would dare insult or attack Israel.

They will know there is a God in Israel!

He'd just defeated the Philistines, he'd crushed Moab and the Arameans under King Hadadezer, and he'd established garrisons in Edom to maintain control of the land. And now, Hanun threw oil on a banked fire. Hanun would burn in the blaze he set!

How long, oh, Lord, how long must I be at war? How long will I have to raise my sword in battle before the nations know there is a God in Israel? I long for peace! I would rather spend my life writing psalms and singing praise to You, my Lord and king, than leading these men of violence into war again. They are too much for me to manage! I'm tired. When will I have rest?

"David," Ahithophel said quietly.

Gritting his teeth, David shut his eyes, struggling for control over his rage and frustration. He knew what his men wanted: war. How they loved battle! How they delighted in shedding blood! Joab and Abishai were like wild donkeys, kicking and fighting the restraints of peace. And many of his mighty men were as bent upon violence as they. They stood restless, discontented with peaceful pursuits, eager to go out into battle where they could unleash their passions. They sought any excuse, and now Hanun had given just cause.

Oh, Lord, how I yearn for the days of my youth!

He wanted to weep as he remembered the freedom of tending his father's flocks. In those days, he had spent countless hours meditating on God's precepts and the Law. He'd walked over pasturelands by day and gazed at the stars by night, experiencing God in everything around him. No one had interfered with his thoughts. No one had distracted him from his praise. Hour after hour, he had delighted in the Lord and felt the presence of God all around him.

Now, burdened with responsibilities, he had to struggle to find time alone. He ached to write psalms for God and set them to the music of his harp. He longed for the days when he'd been no more than a shepherd over his father's flock, responsible merely for finding food and water for his sheep and protecting them from predators. Now, he found himself surrounded by predatory men!

Bowing his head, he gripped the back of his neck. *Oh, Lord! Will there ever be an end to war? I am so tired of living among people who hate peace!*

"Sire," Ahithophel said, stepping closer.

David raised his head. He felt bone weary and depressed. Every decision he made cost human blood. And yet, what other choice had he? He was the king!

"We're going to war again, Ahithophel." He saw the man's dark eyes catch fire. "Come into the inner chamber and we'll discuss it." David motioned to the messenger to approach him. "Joab, Abishai. Both of you as well!" He saw the eagerness in them.

He drew the dusty messenger close. "Rest tonight and then go back. Tell my ambassadors to sojourn in Jericho until their beards grow back."

He was going to make Hanun regret he'd ever laid eyes on them.

+ + +

King Hanun hired Aramean mercenaries to come to his aid, but David went out against them, defeating them and moving on the Ammonites without mercy. They fell by the thousands. The following spring, David gave Joab orders to lay siege to Hanun's city, Rabbah.

Bathsheba stood with her mother at the city gates as the men mustered yet again. David remained astride his mule as he spoke to his commanders and captains. As Uriah stood among them, she felt pride in her husband's position. The thirty mighty men dispersed and returned to their units.

Every time the Ark was carried out of the city and into battle, Bathsheba felt strangely vulnerable. She knew that God could not be put into a box, and yet the Ark represented His presence among the people. And God's presence was going with the army.

Her mother wept when Bathsheba's father marched by. "Each time he leaves, I wonder if I'll ever see him again," she said through her tears. All the women were solemn as fathers, brothers, and husbands went off to war. Bathsheba wept as well. Uriah had given her a home of her own on the street beside the palace, although the palace itself was where he spent most of his time. Sometimes Uriah surprised her with gifts of jewelry to show he loved her. She was proud of the respect he commanded, even more proud that he had earned the respect of her father and grandfather. Many men were courageous in battle, but few had the integrity of her husband. Uriah was a man of his word and a favorite among the king's captains, many of whom had spent an evening in her home, eating a meal she had prepared, while she sat in her private chamber with her maid.

If only she loved him . . . if only she could feel more for him than just affection and respect.

She had only to look at David to know her feelings for him had not diminished with time.

Her mother took her hand. "I pray Uriah will come home to you safely."

"God protect him." She noticed that David was turning his horse away, riding back into the city instead of going out with the men. "David isn't going with them?"

"No. Your grandfather hoped he would change his mind, but David said he's tired, and tired men make poor decisions."

Uriah had said nothing about this.

"You needn't worry about your husband, my dear. Joab and Abishai have proven their ability to command. I suppose the king didn't feel his presence was necessary."

Bathsheba heard the gravity in her mother's voice. Was she criticizing David after all these years of thinking him above reproach? "Is it so wrong for him to remain behind?"

"Unwise. But who am I to say what a king should or shouldn't do?" Her mother turned her face away and spoke wistfully. "If only all men were sick of war! But it seems that will never be. Men live to fight, and women live to bear sons for a king's army."

Bathsheba took her mother's hand and squeezed it. "Perhaps it will not always be so. Perhaps God will allow David to conquer all our enemies and we'll have peace on all sides."

"No good comes from an idle king."

Bathsheba let go of her. "David has never been idle!"

Her mother looked at her. "No, he hasn't. But whom can he conquer inside his own palace walls?" She walked away.

+ + +

The days passed slowly for David. He couldn't recline for a simple meal without hearing constant bickering and whispered complaints from wives and children. His daughters and sons competed for his attention until all he wanted to do was escape to a quiet place and be alone. And when he was alone, restlessness took hold of him. He was discontented and uneasy. Was this all there was to life? He tried to write psalms, but no words would come. Every note he plucked on his lyre was discordant. He tried to rest, but the more he slept, the more tired he felt. Soul tired.

A messenger came with news that Joab and Abishai had defeated the Arameans and were following David's orders to lay siege to Hanun's city, Rabbah. David felt no jubilation. He knew months would pass before the Ammonites would be starved into submission. Attacking the walls might hasten their destruction, but it would needlessly cost lives. He was sick of war!

Bored and melancholy, the king walked the palace walls, gazing out over the city named in his honor, desperate for distraction.

+ + +

The days crawled by as Bathsheba waited for Uriah to come home from the war. When word came that the army had laid siege to Rabbah, she had no illusions that this meant the war was over. Many months could pass before the Ammonites surrendered and Uriah returned home. *If* he returned home. Each time he marched away to war, she lived with the uncertainty that he might be marching out of her life forever, leaving no son behind to carry on his name. She longed to have children. But how could she conceive when her husband was seldom home?

Loneliness became her greatest enemy. It grew to an intolerable ache inside her. Sometimes she sat in the quiet of her chamber and wept over her plight. Yet, what choice had she? Happiness was out of reach.

The city felt empty, populated only by women and children, a few men too old to go into battle, and a king who had decided to remain home, while the war raged on elsewhere.

When she looked up at the wall of David's palace, she imagined him surrounded by doting wives and concubines. A dozen sons and daughters would be delighting him with their attention. Who could be unhappy with so many family members surrounding him? But here she sat, childless and alone, her husband away. How many months had it been since she had laid eyes on Uriah? How many months since she had felt his arms around her? How many more months would come and go, her chance for having a child passing with each one?

She cupped water and pressed it to her flushed cheeks. She knew what was wrong. Every time her menses passed and it was time to take the ritual bath of purification again, self-pity took hold of her. What was the point of making herself ready for a husband who was never home? Another month would pass and another and another, and her arms would remain empty of children. Tears welled. Anger stirred. Frustration abounded.

"Your bath is ready, my lady."

Bathsheba removed her gown and stepped into the basin prepared for her in the privacy of her courtyard. Beneath the gauze canopy that protected her from the harsh afternoon sun, the handmaiden slowly poured water over her body, while Bathsheba washed. She stepped out of the basin and stood waiting as her handmaiden emptied it. Enjoying the coolness of the drying droplets on her body, Bathsheba lifted the heavy mass of curling hair from her back and shoulders. Her handmaiden returned and Bathsheba stepped into the basin again. She drew in her breath as the refreshing water cascaded over her heated flesh. Bathsheba closed her eyes and lifted her head as she stroked the water from her body.

The city was quiet, so quiet she felt a strange sense of expectancy.

Her skin prickled strangely. She sensed someone looking at her. Disturbed, she glanced up and saw a man standing on the wall. Gasping, she covered herself with her hands and ducked beneath the gauzy shelter that did little to hide her. It was afternoon, a time when most people were inside their homes resting and avoiding the heavy heat. What was the man doing on the palace roof?

Angry, she leaned forward to see if she recognized the guard intruding upon her privacy. Uriah would hear of it, and when they returned so would her father and grandfather. As she peered up, her heart jumped.

It was not a palace guard staring down at her, but a man in a white linen tunic with purple trim. *David!*

Her heart pounded as she hid beneath the transparent canopy. Yearning flooded her. Even the sound of the canopy flapping gently in the wind made her senses spin. She remembered how David had looked at her the day she was given to Uriah in marriage and felt all over again the shock of attraction she'd seen in his eyes. If he had noticed her sooner, he could have taken her as his wife instead of looking at her like a starving man.

She knew she should flee to the privacy of the house and complete her bath later, but hurt and resentment filled her. Why not let him see what he had let slip through his fingers? Let him think back to the skinny, sunburned child who had followed him about like an orphaned lamb after its shepherd! She boldly looked up. Would he wish now he'd asked for her instead of leaving it to her father to find a husband for her?

As David stared down, Bathsheba's anger dissolved in a wave of sadness. Why was he standing on the wall and looking down into her courtyard? Why look at her at all with so many beautiful women at his beck and call?

"My lady?"

Startled, Bathsheba turned away, heat surging into her face. Her handmaiden glanced up at the wall. Bathsheba felt a wave of relief when she glanced up and saw that David was no longer there.

"Are you all right, my lady?"

"I was praying." Shame rose inside her. Mortified at what she'd done, she snatched the cloth from the girl, wrapped it around her body, and ran inside the house. Slamming the bedroom door, she leaned against it, holding the damp cloth tightly. She gulped in air as she crossed the room and sank down onto her bed.

What had she done? What could she possibly have been thinking when she allowed the king to gaze upon her? She pressed her hands against her chest, wishing she could calm the wild beating of her heart. Her feelings tumbled one over another—shame, excitement, sorrow, anger, self-loathing. What must David think of her now?

Curling on her side on the bed she shared with her husband, she covered her face and wept.

✦   ✦   ✦

David had seven wives and numerous concubines, and yet, not one could compare in beauty to the woman he had just seen bathing on a rooftop courtyard near the walls of his palace. He had found himself mesmerized by the curves of her body and the grace of every movement. Eve could not have been more perfect!

He knew the moment the woman sensed his presence above her, for she had paused and cocked her head like a hart ready for flight. She looked around slowly and then raised her head. Seeing him on the roof, she drew back quickly beneath the gauzy canopy. For an instant, he was embarrassed to be caught staring at her during such private ablution. But only for a moment. He was the king, after all, and it was his roof. He had every right to stroll it whenever he pleased. She could have bathed inside her house instead of setting up a canopy in her courtyard. What possessed her? His breath had caught in his throat when she looked up at him. He'd never seen a more beautiful woman.

Pushing back from the wall, David strode the battlements until he spotted one of his guards. "Joram!" When the soldier glanced up, David beckoned him.

"My lord the king?"

David took him by the arm and pointed. "There is a woman in that house. Find out who she is."

Startled, the guard quickly left to do his bidding.

David expelled his breath slowly. Gripping the edge of the wall, he watched until the guard appeared on the street below. David turned away and went down the steps hurriedly. Waving away several of his children, he summoned another guard. "When Joram returns, send him to my private chambers immediately."

"Yes, my lord the king."

Alone in his bedroom, David waited. As the minutes passed, he drummed his fingers impatiently. Uneasy, he rose and ran his hand through his hair. He had never felt such fierce desire for a woman. He was troubled, but he chose to ignore the niggling discomfort. Closing his eyes, he imagined the woman again, her small hands open, her head lifted up as though in prayer, and her body, oh, her body. . . .

He bolted from his seat. "What's taking so long?" He paced, agitated and annoyed by the delay. He wanted her and he would have her, whatever the cost.

Someone tapped at the door. "Enter!" Joram stood on the threshold. "Come in and close the door behind you." David waited, hands on his hips. "What did you find out?"

"The woman's name is Bathsheba."

"Bathsheba?" Why did that name sound so familiar? "Bathsheba . . ."

"She is Bathsheba, the daughter of Eliam and the wife of Uriah the Hittite."

Oh no! David felt his stomach drop. He remembered a skinny little girl who used to sit on Ahithophel's knee and stare at him across the fire. No! It couldn't be! Little Bathsheba, who, as a child, had worshiped him and followed him to the stream at En-gedi. *"I want to talk with you."* Her heart had been in her eyes. Bathsheba, married to one of his best and most reliable friends, daughter of a man he trusted and who trusted him, granddaughter of Ahithophel, Israel's most able military adviser. Could anything be worse? He remembered looking into her eyes on her wedding day and feeling as though someone had punched him in the stomach. He'd made sure from that day on never to look at her again!

He expelled a hoarse laugh. Turning, he gripped the back of his neck. The old weariness and depression rose up once again. "You may go, Joram."

"Is there anything you wish for, my lord the king?"

David clenched his teeth. "Nothing I can have."

"Nothing is out of your reach, Sire. You are the *king*. Whatever you want is yours."

David lowered his hand and raised his head. He *was* the king. Furthermore, his army was miles away at Rabbah. Uriah, Eliam, and Ahithophel had been gone for months and would not return for many more to come. His heart began to pound. What if he did summon Bathsheba to his private chambers? What if they did find pleasure in one another's arms? What harm could one night do? Who would ever know?

His desire for Bathsheba burned hotter.

"What is your wish, Sire?"

"Bring her to me." He felt a pang of guilt as he spoke his lust aloud, but he quickly squelched it with thoughts of the night ahead. Still, he must be prudent. "Wait until dark before you go for her, and take another soldier you know can keep a secret."

"And if the woman resists?"

"She won't." Bathsheba had loved him for years. She'd followed him around the camps at Adullam and En-gedi. He'd thought she was a pesky little fly then, but now . . .

"But if she does . . . ?"

She was a common woman and he was a king. "My order stands." Joram bowed and left. David knew Bathsheba would come to him. She had been extending him an invitation when she had so boldly met his eyes during her bath. If she regretted her impulse, he would take pleasure in swaying her.

It would be hours yet before Bathsheba was brought to his bedchamber. Time enough to bathe and anoint himself with scented oils. Time enough to order a small feast prepared. Time enough to burn incense to tease her senses. Time enough to think about the pleasures of the night ahead.

Time enough for sin to conquer him.

✦   ✦   ✦

Bathsheba spent the rest of the afternoon in her chamber, weeping and wondering how she would ever have the courage to show her face before the king again. She dressed in a loose embroidered robe that hid every curve of her body. She brushed her hair until her scalp hurt. Then, holding the brush against her chest, she rocked and sobbed. Time hadn't dissolved her love for David. This afternoon when she realized he was the one on the roof looking down at her, all the old feelings had risen up and swept over her again.

Someone tapped at her door. "My lady?" came the muffled voice of her maid.

"Go away!"

"There's a soldier at the door, my lady!" The girl's voice was shaking with alarm. "He said you must come!"

A soldier? Bathsheba rose quickly. She could think of only one reason a soldier would come to her door. Uriah was wounded or dead! Uttering a sob, Bathsheba threw open her door, brushed past her maid, and hurried through the house, her handmaiden on her heels.

The soldier stood just inside her door, but he wasn't dusty from travel. And he wore a palace guard's uniform. Startled, Bathsheba stopped. "Why are you here?"

The corner of his mouth turned up. "The king has summoned you, Lady Bathsheba."

"Summoned me?" Confused, she stared back at him. "The king?"

"Yes. *The king.*" He stepped back and extended his hand toward the open front door. Another soldier was standing outside looking in at her. Bathsheba began to shake. She was a little girl again, crouching behind a boulder as David reprimanded her. Her cheeks caught fire.

"My lady." The handmaiden moaned. "Oh, my lady."

Bathsheba turned to her quickly and grasped her hands. "Hush, now. The king won't harm me, Hatshepsut. He's known my father and grandfather for many years." Could that be the reason he was summoning her? "Perhaps he has news of them. Go quickly and bring me my shawl." The girl ran to do her bidding while Bathsheba stood, filled with anxiety, before the palace guard. His hand rested on the hilt of his sword as he waited, head up, eyes straight ahead. Was it bad news from Rabbah? "Has the king summoned my mother as well?" Why would the king bother himself to personally inform two women they had lost loved ones in the war?

"Your mother?" The guard spoke wryly. "I think not."

"Then can you tell me why the king wishes to see me?"

He looked at her then, and the expression in his eyes made heat rise into her cheeks again.

Her handmaiden returned with a shawl. Heart pounding, Bathsheba took it and draped it over her head and across one shoulder so that her face wouldn't be seen. As she went out the door, the guards fell in on either side of her. It didn't occur to her until she was near the palace entrance that she was still wearing the loose embroidered robe she normally wore only inside her own house.

"This way!" The guard jerked his head and led her toward a pathway around to a side entrance used only by servants. If there had been any question in her mind as to the clandestine reason for the king's summons, or her social standing in his eyes, she had none now. Tears of shame pricked her eyes. She had only herself to blame for this situation. She kept her head down and her face covered as she went in through the servants' entrance. She walked through the palace kitchen, the servants' quarters and corridors, and up a flight of stairs, looking neither to the right nor the left. The guards stopped before a door. One knocked lightly, and the other stood to one side.

The moment the door opened and Bathsheba looked up, she forgot all about the guards. David's gaze was fixed upon her.

When he smiled and held out his hand, she took it, her breath catching when his fingers closed warm and firm around hers. He drew her into his private chamber as he gave orders to the guard to keep watch. "No one is to disturb me." And then David closed the door behind her. Her heart leaped and bounded like a rabbit fleeing for its life. He still had hold of her hand, and there seemed to be no indication that he intended to let go. "I'm glad you came."

"Did I have any choice?"

"You did choose."

He kissed her hand, his eyes smiling into hers. "Why do you cover your face, when you're more beautiful than the sun or the moon?"

When she raised her hand to hold her shawl in place, he inclined his head slightly. "Come. I've had a meal prepared for us. Let me serve you."

The air was filled with the sweet scent of incense. Cushions were scattered on the floor. A large bed loomed across the room. Food was spread over a long table. "How many were you expecting?"

He laughed, and the throaty sound made her tremble. "Only you, my sweet."

"I'm not very hungry." Gathering her courage, she looked at him. "Do you know who I am?"

"Of course." His eyes caressed her face. "You're the little girl who used to stare across the fire at me. Do you remember following me to the stream at En-gedi?"

"I'm not a little girl anymore. I'm—"

"The most beautiful woman in the kingdom." David searched her eyes. "You said you wanted to talk to me that morning. I told you to go home." He tucked his finger into her shawl and drew it down from her face. "Talk to me now, Bathsheba." He stepped closer and lifted the shawl from her hair. "Say whatever is on your mind." The shawl slipped down from her shoulders and pooled around her feet.

"Why do you call for me *now*?" Her voice was thick with tears. All the years she had dreamed and hoped. She had never wanted to come to him like this. Summoned in the middle of the night . . .

"You know." He breathed against her neck.

Her skin tingled. "It's too late."

"You're here with me now."

She drew back and lifted her chin, scarcely able to see his face through her tears. "Summoned like a harlot and brought to you through the servants' gate!" She shook her head and bowed her head again. "And I've no one else to blame, considering the way I behaved this afternoon. I'm sorry. I—"

"You took my breath away."

"I did?" Her child's heart trembled and swelled with pride. "Oh, David. Send me back."

"Not yet." He tipped her chin firmly. "You aren't happy, are you?"

Tears trickled down her cheeks. "How can you ask such a question?"

"I want you to be happy." He searched her eyes and his expression changed. He looked troubled. "Do you remember your wedding feast? When I looked into your eyes in Hebron, my stomach dropped to my feet. I couldn't take my eyes off you."

"Is that why you left so quickly?"

"Why else?" He put his arms around her.

She put her hands against his chest. She knew she should say something to stop him. She should be like Abigail and make him aware of the sin he was about to commit. But her resolve weakened when she felt his heart pounding faster and harder than her own. He wanted her. *I'll let him kiss me once, just once, and then I'll say something to stop him. I'll have his kiss to remember. Just one.*

When his mouth took hers, Bathsheba felt herself being pulled down with him into a vortex of desire. His fingers raked through her hair. He moaned her name, and the words of warning died in her throat. As her body caught fire, she clung to him and didn't say a word.

She knew that if she did, David would remember himself and send her home where she belonged.

+   +   +

Hours later, David stood beside his bed watching Bathsheba sleep. She was so beautiful she made his heart ache. But it would be dawn soon. He had to get her out of the palace before anyone knew she'd been here. When he'd awakened and seen her lying beside him, he thought of Ahithophel, Eliam, and Uriah, and what they would make of this clandestine affair. *What was I thinking! They could turn the army against me!*

Putting his knee on the bed, he leaned down and kissed her. Her eyes opened slowly, still clouded with sleep. She smiled. "David," she sighed.

His pulse quickened. Shaken by his feelings, he straightened. "It's almost daylight, Bathsheba. You have to go."

Her smile died.

David's stomach squeezed tight at the wounded look in her eyes. Turning quickly away, she dragged a blanket up and covered herself. Shame hadn't been in attendance last night, only unbridled passion. But now, morning had come and light streamed in upon the true situation.

"My guards will see you safely back to your house." Why should he feel guilty? They had a right to some happiness, didn't they?

She sat up quickly. "I know my way home." When he heard the soft sound she made as she groped for her discarded robe, he went down on his knees on the bed and reached for her.

"Bathsheba," he said, his voice hoarse with pent-up emotion. She jerked from his touch. He caught hold of her shoulders and pulled her back against him. She struggled to be free. He locked his arms around her. "Bathsheba," he said raggedly and buried his face in her neck. How could he let her go after last night? He breathed in the scent of her and knew he was undone.

"I thought last night would be enough." She put the heels of her hands against her eyes. "I thought I could live on the memories of being with you. But now . . . I feel . . . I feel . . . unclean!" She shuddered.

Her words so mirrored his own feelings that he was

disturbed. "Do you think I *want* to send you away?" He felt torn and frustrated. "I'd keep you with me if it wouldn't raise a cry across the city. Your father . . . your grandfather."

"My husband!"

"I have to get you out of here before anyone knows what's happened between us."

Her body was tense against him. When he kissed her neck, she leaned her head back with a shaky sigh. "It's no use. Someone will find out. And I'll die for it."

He went rigid. "No one's going to find out!"

She turned in his arms, and he saw the fear in her eyes. "People already know, David! Your guards, my handmaiden. Any one of a dozen people who saw your men bring me in through the servants' entrance last night."

He dug his fingers into her hair. "And who are they to dare speak against the king? My men will keep silent, and you will tell your maid she'd better hold her tongue if she values her life!" He saw the shock in her eyes and spoke more gently. "You didn't realize what a ruthless man I could be, did you?" He tried to smile, but there was a fierceness inside him that claimed her for his own. "Listen, my love. Suppose someone did whisper of our night together. Would any priest dare confront me?"

"Nathan would."

"Nathan knows me. He would dismiss any gossip as ugly rumor and nothing more. And besides, who would take the word of a guard or handmaiden over that of a king?" He kissed her tears away. "Trust me. I won't allow any harm to come to you. I swear it!"

"I've always trusted you, David. My father said you've always been a man of your word."

David winced inwardly, but anger rose quickly in self-defense. Why should he feel guilty over spending one night with the woman he desired? What harm could come of something done in secret? He was the king. Didn't he deserve some happiness? Kings had always taken whomever they wanted. Why shouldn't he? Who had done more in bringing the tribes together? Who had killed Goliath and rallied the Israelite army to victory? Who had led the kingdom to victory after victory? Who had been wrongly accused and pursued for years all because the people loved him? And during those hard years, who had been the one man to praise God? Besides, it was no one's business but his own what he did in the privacy of his chamber!

Still, he knew it was wiser to keep his own counsel in this particular matter. He thought of Eliam, his longtime friend. He thought of Ahithophel, his adviser. He thought of Uriah's courage and ferocity in battle. If they found out Bathsheba had spent the night in his bed, there would be trouble. All three were men of God and would want to follow the letter of the Law. And the Law of Moses demanded that an adulteress be put to death.

Fear gripped David's belly as he realized the danger to Bathsheba. He shoved it away and reminded himself he was the king! Who would dare touch a woman he loved?

"No stone will ever strike you." He would kill any man who tried to harm her.

It never once occurred to David that it was he who was shattering her life.

✦ ✦ ✦

Bathsheba waited for David to summon her again, but he didn't. She watched for him on the wall, but the king didn't appear. She listened for word of him, but all she heard was "The king is resting in his palace while our husbands are off at Rabbah fighting his war with the Ammonites!"

"It's our war," she said in his defense. "If the Ammonites get away with insulting David's ambassadors, they might think him weak and attack Jerusalem. Better to have the battle at Rabbah than here."

She tried to tell herself that David was busy with matters of state, but jealousy and hurt crept in. Her imagination tormented her. *Whom is he holding in his arms tonight? Ahinoam? Abigail?* Or had he lost all interest in his wives and concubines? *How many other women in this city have looked up at the handsome king strolling along the battlements and yearned to warm his bed?* She remembered the girls in the camps, girls exactly like her, who'd gazed at David with adoring eyes and dreamed dreams about him.

David could have anyone he wanted! Even before he was king, women were falling in love with him.

She was stricken with regret and fear as the days passed. If only she had fled to the privacy of her house that day. If only she hadn't brazenly continued her bath, exposing herself to this endless heartache. She had no one to blame but herself for what she suffered now. She'd gone willingly to David's bed. She'd told herself love was reason enough to give herself to him. David, her god.

Why hadn't she thought about the Law before she gave herself to him? He had assured her that no stone would touch her. But what could he do if the priests cried out against her? For if their affair became known, she had no illusions about who would bear the blame. David was a beloved king. She was a powerless woman.

Adultery! She'd committed adultery! How could she have done such a thing after being brought up by her mother, father, and grandfather, who all held to the Law of Moses with such fierce devotion?

If they ever find out, they'll kill me!

A week passed and then another and another, and she received no summons from the palace, no message, no hint of David's concern. How easily he had abandoned her!

The time for her monthly show of blood came and went, and terror filled her. After all the years of trying and failing to conceive with Uriah, she was pregnant after one night in David's arms! Why now? Why under these circumstances? What could she do now?

Had she only imagined the tenderness in David's touch? Had her hope deceived her into believing she saw love in his eyes? If he loved her, wouldn't he have summoned her by now? or at the least have sent a message of some kind?

Nothing! He cares nothing about me!

She pressed her hands against her temples. Seven wives and ten concubines! What need had he of her? Would he even care that she was with child as a result of her night with him? In a few months, everyone was going to know she'd committed adultery. Her handmaiden had already guessed she was pregnant—and by whom. Soon her mother would notice the changes in her. Soon every man, woman, and child who laid eyes upon her would guess her secret.

Trembling, she placed her hands on her abdomen. She was torn between terror and exultation. Within her womb was the child of a king—not just any king, but King David, hero of her childhood dreams. David, singer of songs, conqueror of nations! He had been like a god to her.

Anger filled her. She looked up at the wall of his palace where David had stood on that fateful day of her undoing. She'd always thought she would rejoice when she was with child, eagerly anticipating the happy event of bearing a son to her patient, loving husband.

Never in her life had she felt such despair and fear!

Was it the love she'd felt for David all these years that had made the soil fertile enough to accept the seed?

Only the king could protect her from suffering the consequences of their sin.

But would he?

She grieved over David's silence and was terrified at what Uriah would do to her when he found out how she'd betrayed him. What defense had she? David hadn't dragged her into the palace kicking and screaming!

She'd never wanted to hurt Uriah. He was a good man, a kind and generous husband. But Uriah's touch didn't make her burn. David's embrace made her soar and melt. Was it so wrong to crave the caresses of a man she'd loved for as long as she could remember? Wasn't she entitled to one night of happiness without having her entire life destroyed by it?

Life was unfair!

She'd never been meant for Uriah. She'd been meant for David. Surely that made it all right for them to steal a few hours together. She'd thought she would have wonderful memories of their night together, enough to last a lifetime, but she was tormented instead. The fire David had built in her was turning her life to ashes. She felt abandoned and terrified of the future. She'd been filled up with love for him. She'd poured herself out like a drink offering for David, her king. David, her idol. And now, she was consumed by fear, her loneliness worse than ever. It was too late to go back and undo anything. What price would she pay for that one night? What cost to others whom she loved and who loved her? Uriah, her mother, her father, her grandfather. She couldn't bear to think of it. She would rather die than have them know. But did she have the courage to take her own life?

Shaking, she put her hands over her belly again. If she died, so would David's child. Part of her rejoiced over the life growing within her. Part of her wished the evidence of her sin would be swept from her body with a stream of blood before anyone else knew of it. Everyone was going to know this child was conceived in adultery. How could she defend herself when her husband had been away at war for months? She imagined the angry shouts of a mob closing around her, taking up stones. She imagined the condemnation in her mother's eyes, the hurt, the disappointment. A mother knew a daughter's heart better than anyone. Her mother had known for years that she was in love with David. Hadn't she counseled Bathsheba to give up her childish fantasies, her unrequited love? Hadn't her mother told her to guard her heart? The blame wouldn't be put at the feet of the king, but laid firmly upon her head.

No one could help her now. No one but David. But would he?

Lowering her hands, she clenched them in her lap. Silence did not always mean indifference. Hadn't he promised that no harm would come to her? Hadn't he sworn it? Hadn't David always been a man of his word?

She cut a piece of papyrus from Uriah's accounts. David would help her. He had to help her! She wrote him a brief message. Rolling it tightly, she tied a string around it. Then she summoned her handmaiden. "Take this to the king."

"What if the guards won't let me through the gate?"

"Ask for Joram. Give him the message. Tell him it's from me and meant for the king's eyes only."

"Yes, my lady."

Bathsheba closed the door and pressed her forehead against it. All types of fearsome possibilities swirled in her mind. Surely David would be honor bound to help her. Surely he wouldn't forsake the daughter of Eliam, the granddaughter of Ahithophel. Surely he would try to do something for her so that Uriah would never find out she'd betrayed him. But what could he do? What? He could secret her away so that she could have his child in another city. Where would he send her? Where? Where!

Oh, David, help me! Please help me!

She refused to believe he was indifferent. How could he be after the risks he'd taken to bring her into the palace? But what would David do to solve this problem?

Exhausted by worry, she sat. She had no choice but to wait, for her life was in the king's hands.

+ + +

David felt an ominous premonition when his guard whispered, "The handmaid of Bathsheba, wife of Uriah, has come with a message." The mere mention of Bathsheba's name was a jolt to his senses, arousing feelings he knew were better forgotten. He'd never wanted a woman as much as he wanted her. How many times over the past weeks had he denied himself the pleasure of summoning her again because he knew it would increase the risk of exposure? He'd had to remind himself repeatedly that she was the wife of a friend, the daughter of one of his most valued captains, the granddaughter of Ahithophel, a man he'd respected for years! He had enough trouble in the kingdom without turning friends into enemies!

"Bring the maidservant to me."

He felt curious eyes upon him as he untied the string around the small papyrus. He read Bathsheba's brief message, and his stomach dropped. Heat climbed up his neck and spread across his face. Three words, enough to shock him from his complacency and trumpet disaster:

I am pregnant.

He felt the accusation in those three words and heard Bathsheba's desperate cry for help. He brushed his fingers lightly over the words and frowned. Guilt gripped him.

Oh, Bathsheba. He remembered his promise and wondered how he could fulfill it. Her handmaiden stood in the doorway, waiting for his reply. He saw heads leaning toward one another, whispering. Speculation already! He could hear the soft buzz. Would it grow into screams for blood? His *and* hers? Disaster stretched ahead for both of them if word of their affair spread. He needed time to think, time to find a solution to this problem!

Crumpling Bathsheba's message in his hand, he leaned back indolently and smiled, beckoning forward the next person who had come to present a case before the king. He listened impatiently and made a decision he saw was ill received. What did he care about their petty differences when Bathsheba faced certain death? He had to find a way to rescue her from the dire situation she was in. If he didn't find a way to cover their sin, there would be trouble in the ranks of his fighting men. They would lose faith in him, possibly rebel.

"Enough!" He stood. He waved his servants away. "I need to be alone."

When he entered his chamber, he closed the door and put Bathsheba's crumpled message in among the embers of burning incense, watching as it burned.

He sat for an hour with his head in his hands before a plan came to him. He knew it would save them both from exposure and would even give cause for celebration among his closest friends. He smiled at his own cleverness as he summoned Joram.

"Send a messenger to Rabbah and tell Joab to send me Uriah the Hittite."

Joram bowed and left.

Strangely agitated, David removed his crown and tossed it on his bed. He raked his fingers back through his hair. Temptation gripped him to summon Bathsheba and explain his plan, but he squelched the impulse. Why take any more risks when, in less than a week's time, there would be no cause for fear of reprisals? Uriah would return to Jerusalem, where his king would treat him with the respect of an emissary. David intended to find out what was happening at Rabbah.

And then he would send the Hittite home to his wife.

Bathsheba was the granddaughter of Ahithophel. Surely she would be quick to see the means of her salvation and fulfill her part in the plan. He would even send food and wine as reward for Uriah's service. Any man who'd been gone as long as Uriah would be eager for his wife.

David clenched a fist as jealousy gripped him. The plan was repugnant, but he could see no flaw in it. Whatever he felt now about Bathsheba's lying with another man, the act would save her life as well as that of his child. The plan would also save him embarrassment. If all went accordingly, Uriah would never know he'd been betrayed by his wife and cuckolded by a friend. David found grudging satisfaction in knowing that this child of his loins would be brought up by an honorable man who had adopted the ways of Israel.

He relaxed his fist and sighed heavily. He would allow the Hittite *one* night to get the deed done, and then he'd order him back to his duties at Rabbah. In a few weeks, Bathsheba could send word to her husband that she was with child, and Uriah could celebrate with his friends in the army while finishing the job of taking Rabbah.

The matter thus resolved in his mind, David stretched out on his bed and slept for the rest of the afternoon.

✦ ✦ ✦

When her maid opened the door at last, Bathsheba jumped to her feet. "What news?"

The girl's eyes flickered in discomfort. "The guard took me to the king's court."

"The king's court?" Bathsheba felt weak and light-headed. How many courtiers had been in attendance when her message was delivered? How many tongues were now wagging with speculations? She didn't ask. She didn't want to know.

"Joram demanded to know who had sent me." Her hand-maiden started to weep. "I had to tell him, my lady. I had to. But I said it quietly. I said it so quietly, he had to bend forward and tell me to repeat what I'd said. And then he went forward and informed the king."

"For all to hear?"

The girl's face was pale. "No. He whispered into the king's ear."

Somehow that made everything worse. Bathsheba shuddered. "Did Joram take my message?"

"Yes, my lady."

"Did he give it to David?"

"Yes, my lady."

"And did the king summon you then? Did he give you a message to bring back to me? Did he say *anything* to you?"

"No, my lady, no, no—but how could he say anything with so many around to hear and wonder? He called for . . ."

"Called for . . . ?"

"The next case."

Bathsheba turned her face away. "You may go."

"Oh, my lady . . ."

"Go!"

Alone, Bathsheba sank to the floor and covered her face.

It was too late to regret loving David, too late to regret giving herself to him without a word of protest. All she could do now was wait and see if David would remember his promise to her.

For now, it appeared he'd chosen to remember her not at all.

three

DAVID assessed Uriah as the soldier approached the throne. He was a tall man with broad shoulders, his skin weathered and ruddy from years in the sun, his mouth an uncompromising line. He'd removed his leather helmet and tucked it beneath one of his arms. David noticed the streaks of gray at the Hittite's temples. He stopped in front of the throne, hit his fist against his heart, and bowed low before David. "My lord the king!"

When the Hittite straightened, David inclined his head with the respect due a man of proven loyalty and courage, well respected by captains as well as commanders, and even the king. No sign of curiosity lit Uriah's eyes now. He was a consummate soldier, who obeyed his supreme commander without question. David knew that whatever he commanded, Uriah would do.

Relaxing, David leaned back. This was going to be easy. "How does Joab fare? Tell me about the people and how the war prospers."

"All goes well, my lord the king." Uriah gave detailed information on how Joab and Abishai had employed the captains and the soldiers beneath their command. Uriah gave a full picture of the situation. He spoke of skirmishes in which the Ammonites had been chased back inside the city "like dogs with their tails between their legs." David laughed with him. Uriah spoke of the fear upon the land since David had defeated Hadadezer and his allies the previous year. "Hanun is alone. It's only a matter of time before Rabbah falls and Hanun's crown will be placed in your hands."

Nodding, David smiled. "Good news, indeed. Is it not so?" He looked around at the other men in court who received the news eagerly. He returned his attention to Uriah. The time to show magnanimity was right. "You may take your leave, my friend. Go on home and relax."

A frown flickered across Uriah's brow. "My lord the king!" With a fist against his heart, he bowed low again, straightened, stepped back, and turned with the precision of a marching man. David stifled his jealousy as he watched the Hittite stride from the throne room.

"Joram." He beckoned his guard. "I want a meal prepared for Uriah and his wife, something special, something that will bring back fond memories of their wedding feast." He gripped the arms of his throne tightly. "Have it prepared and delivered to Uriah's house immediately."

"Yes, my lord the king."

Good food would help Uriah relax and make the transition from battlefield to a peaceful night in the arms of his beautiful young wife.

David spent the rest of the day hearing various cases brought before him by the people. The trifling disputes tried his patience, but the time he spent resolving them kept him from dwelling upon the thought of Bathsheba in the arms of another man.

He would give Uriah one night to do what was expected, and then the man was going back to Joab at Rabbah.

✦   ✦   ✦

Bathsheba was feverish when her mother greeted her in the marketplace with news that Uriah had been seen entering Jerusalem. "He must have news from Rabbah," her mother said, going on to make a dozen speculations while Bathsheba felt the sweat break out on her body. What could David possibly be thinking? Was he going to confess to her husband? Would he claim she'd seduced him by parading naked in front of him? Or had he other plans? Would he offer gifts to absolve his guilt? She told her mother she wanted to prepare to see her husband and hurried home, where she remained, pacing in agitation.

When Joram and several servants of the king came to her house laden with trays of succulent food, enough quantity and variety to please a king, she was alarmed. "What is all this?" Surely David wasn't intending to come into her house. Her neighbors would see and talk. The whole city would know of their affair!

"Tell Uriah that the king sends his best wishes for a pleasant evening," Joram said with a mocking smile.

"Uriah has been serving in Rabbah."

"Indeed, until he was summoned from Rabbah to report to the king about the war. My lord the king gave him leave to return home and spend the night with you."

She felt the heat come up from her toes to the top of her head as she understood the full implication of what Joram was saying. "Uriah isn't here." And even if he had come home, he would not put a hand upon her. Did David know his men so little? Had he forgotten the Law? When a man was called out to war, he was to remain abstinent from sexual relations. He was to save his strength for battle against the enemies of Israel rather than spend it on his own pleasure.

"Then I will find him," Joram said. "I will inform him of what the king has done to honor him." He waved the servants out and left.

Honor Uriah? Shame swept over Bathsheba as she realized the way David had chosen to help her. He was attempting to hide their sin of adultery by enticing her husband to sleep with her and believe he was the father of her child! Was this the fulfillment of David's promise to help her? He was drawing her into deeper sin, pulling her down further into sorrow and shame. If Uriah gave in to his fleshly nature, David expected her to lie and pretend to rejoice that she was with child, for everyone would naturally assume the child was Uriah's. Uriah would have to bear the embarrassment of having broken his vow of abstinence.

Oh, she saw everything so clearly now. David, commander of the army of Israel, rested in his palace while his army fought the war. The king, restless and bored, peeping

at her as she bathed and summoning her for his own pleasure. He hadn't cared that she belonged to another man,
a man who'd been his friend through the hard years of
running from King Saul, a man of proven loyalty, a man
both valorous and honorable! And she had gone to him, her
heart in her hands, giving everything of value to him. She'd
prostituted herself to her idol-king, who took his leisure
while men like her husband risked their lives to win his
battles against Israel's enemies!

How would she face Uriah when he came home? How
would she look into his eyes and survive the anguish? How
could she have betrayed him like this? She'd succumbed to
her childish fantasies and made a fool of herself, imagining
that one night of passion meant anything lasting to a king!
She'd served to sate his desire for a night. She meant nothing to him. He'd probably forgotten all about her until she
sent him that message! Did he curse the inconvenience of
her conception?

"What have I done?" She groaned, her arms hugging
herself as she rocked back and forth. "What have I done?"

Joram returned. "Your husband is sitting at the door of
the king's house with all the servants of David. I told him of
what the king sent in his honor." He stepped forward. "You
must go to Uriah, my lady. Go to him and do whatever you
must to bring your husband home to you for the night. It is
the king's wish that you do so."

The king's wish.

If she fulfilled her part in the abominable plan, the king's
reputation would be unblemished by scandal, she would
live, the child would live, and Uriah would never know the

truth. She could go on pretending she was the dutiful, loving, faithful wife. She could have the child she'd longed for. The people would be spared the same anguish she now felt, realizing the man she'd loved and worshiped for so many years was deeply flawed. He was no longer the charismatic boy who had killed Goliath and rallied the nation. He was a king whom power had corrupted, for he had become selfish, cunning, and capable of deceit.

Bathsheba felt unclean and helpless. David was presenting her with a way to survive. If she didn't go through with it, she'd die. So would the child she carried.

"Go," she said softly. "Just go and leave me to do what I must." She closed the door behind Joram. Dismissing her maid for the night, she took up her shawl and went out of the house. She stood in the darkness for a long time, feeling it press in around her. She wished she could think of another way out of the mess she'd stepped into when she had freely allowed the king to gaze upon her in her bath. As she walked along the moonlit street, she looked up at the wall of the palace where David had stood gazing down at her as she bathed. And she realized, even now, her feelings for him hadn't changed. How was it possible, with her eyes wide open, that she could still love David so much?

She saw the palace gate, closed for the night. Guards were still posted. She approached slowly, her heart in her throat. Would they ask her name, ask her purpose in coming? Or would they be among the many soldiers she'd met at her father's campfire, or who served in the house of her husband?

Two soldiers stepped forward. "Woman, why do you come at this hour?"

"I am Bathsheba, wife of Uriah. I was told my husband has returned from Rabbah."

"Uriah is bedded down inside the gate with the king's servants. He is among *friends*."

She felt the cold wind blowing.

Did men talk among themselves as women did? Were rumors circulating among the palace servants? Even if they were, who would dare tell Uriah that his friend, the king, had cuckolded him?

"I will tell him you're here," the other guard said and left them. The guard who had spoken first returned to his position without a word. He didn't look at her. Bathsheba understood the implications of his rudeness. He knew about her affair with the king.

How many others knew?

She kept her face covered as she waited. The city slept and only the guard was present, but she could feel eyes upon her, eyes that saw through her subterfuge and into her heart. She wanted to cower and hide, but knew she would never escape.

The gate was opening. The guard reappeared and her husband followed.

As Uriah walked toward her, her heart hammered. She turned slightly and took a few steps away from the gate so they would have privacy to talk. When he stopped before her, she raised her eyes and saw his troubled expression. He searched her face intently, but didn't speak.

"The king sent a feast to our house to welcome you home." Her voice trembled.

His eyes flickered, and then an expression spread across his face that made her go cold. Something had been confirmed. His face went taut as though he had been struck. "So," he said and said no more.

He knew!

She saw the moist sheen build in his eyes and wanted to curl up at his feet and die. Could anything hurt a man more than to learn the wife he loved had betrayed him in another man's bed—especially that of a king he'd loved so much and served so long? She might as well have drawn Uriah's sword from his belt and stabbed him through the heart. Her throat closed tight and hot. *What can I do? How can I show him how sorry I am?* Her hands relaxed, and the shawl slipped down around her shoulders as her eyes filled with tears. "Oh, Uriah . . ." She could say no more. She shook with sorrow and shame.

"They expect me to kill you where you stand," he said hoarsely.

"And so you should." What excuse had she? What defense could she offer? As much as David's callow treatment hurt her, she couldn't cast all the blame at his feet. She'd been willing and eager for him. Now she saw the cost to a man who truly loved her. Heartsick, she went down on her knees and found a stone large enough to fill her palm. Straightening, she extended her hand. "You have every right."

A muscle jerked in his jaw as tears spilled down his cheeks and into his beard. He took the stone and made

a fist. She could see him struggling with his emotions. After
a long moment, he shook his head and dropped the stone at
her feet. When he lifted his hand, she waited for the blow,
but he merely laid his hand gently against her cheek. He
stroked her tear-dampened skin with his thumb as he gazed
into her eyes, his own filled with sorrow and forgiveness.
She put her hand over his and closed her eyes in anguish,
and felt him slip his hand from beneath hers.

She watched him walk slowly away, his shoulders bent.
A guard opened the palace gate just enough for him to pass
through to the inner gate, where he would spend the night
with other soldiers like himself, men who had dedicated
their lives to the service of the king. Then the gate was
closed behind him, and the guards resumed their posts.

Bathsheba never saw Uriah again.

✦   ✦   ✦

David clenched the arms of his throne. "What do you mean,
Uriah spent the night with my servants at the gate?" He
strove to keep his voice calm while his insides tensed and
roiled in anger as he thought of the hours of torment he'd
suffered the night before, imagining that Hittite caressing
Bathsheba. How dare Uriah disobey his command! "I told
him he could go down to his house."

"He slept with your servants at the gate, my lord the
king."

"Bring him to me." When the servant left, David fought
to regain control of his emotions so that others in the court
wouldn't be curious over his reaction. He would be magnan-
imous and give the Hittite another opportunity to make
things right.

When Uriah entered the court, David dismissed the others and smiled as Uriah walked forward. "What is this I hear, my friend?" he said in the cajoling manner of two men who had been friends for years. "What's the matter with you? Why didn't you go home last night after being away for so long?"

Uriah's dark eyes were inscrutable. "The Ark and the armies of Israel and Judah are living in tents, and Joab and his officers are camping in the open fields. How could I go home to wine and dine and sleep with my wife? I swear that I will never be guilty of acting like that."

David felt the heat come up into his face. Was the Hittite reprimanding him? Was he saying that the Ark and the army were encamped in tents while the king was at his leisure inside his palace walls? David felt the sting of reproach. Breathing slowly to cool the hot blood racing through his veins, he leaned back and considered Uriah. "Well, stay here tonight, and tomorrow you may return to the army."

Uriah turned.

David's teeth clenched as he watched Uriah walk from the throne room. The Hittite hadn't addressed him properly as "my lord the king." Had the soldier forgotten to make obeisance? Or had the omission been deliberate?

Joram reported on Uriah's movements the next morning. The Hittite remained in Jerusalem as commanded, but did not go down to his house. Impatient and frustrated, David ordered a sumptuous feast prepared for two and summoned Uriah to be his guest. He sat on the dais, eating and drinking before the Hittite, encouraging the Hittite to do likewise. Food and drink always relaxed a man and helped turn his thoughts to other sensual delights. The evening proved torturous, for Uriah scorned food while he drank freely and talked—talked of the glorious battles they'd fought together. His words were like bee stings, pricking David's conscience and swelling his resentment. He didn't need to be reminded of how the mighty men had served him. But who had led them? David had! The mighty men would have been no more than a band of marauders without him!

Raising his cup, Uriah toasted David. "To the shepherd boy we made a king." He wept as he drained his cup.

David was disgusted by the man's display of emotion. The Hittite couldn't hold his wine. David was eager to see the back of him. He rose and came down from his dais. Gripping the Hittite's arm, he hauled him to his feet. "Enough for tonight, my old friend." He slapped his back. "Go home."

David watched him walk unsteadily from the chamber.

Joram came to him shortly afterward. "He sleeps at the gate, my lord the king."

"I'll deal with him in the morning." Angry, David retired, but his sleep was troubled. Someone was trying to speak to him, and he knew he didn't want to hear what the Voice had to say. Groaning, he awakened drenched with sweat. He sat on the edge of the bed he'd shared with Bathsheba and thought of the promise he'd made. He lowered his head and held it between his hands. Uriah hadn't cooperated, so he would have to think of another way to help her. A pity the Hittite hadn't been killed at Rabbah. Then there'd be no problem. He could . . .

His head came up. Another plan developed, one final and perfect, and one that would give him what he wanted most: Bathsheba.

David rose and went to the writing table, where he had composed some of his most beautiful psalms. He prepared the ink in its small pot, dipped his brush, and began to write orders for Joab, commander of his army: *"Station Uriah on the front lines where the battle is fiercest. Then pull back so that he will be killed."*

David knew that Joab, of all men, would understand the need for secrecy. He would also understand the passions of a man's heart. After all, Joab had once murdered a man in vengeance. He would do whatever David told him without question—and without condemnation. In fact, he would probably admire the king's cunning.

Rolling the small scroll, David melted wax and pressed his ring into it to seal the message. Then he rose, washed, dressed, and went to the court. "Bring me Uriah the Hittite."

Within a matter of minutes, Uriah entered the courtroom. David saw that he had washed as well. He walked forward with regal bearing, displaying no sign of ill effects from the night of drinking. He stopped before the throne, but he said nothing. Nor did he bend his knee or put his fist against his chest and bow as he had done the day of his arrival. He stood silent, waiting.

David held out the small sealed scroll. "Give this to Joab." His heart beat ten times before Uriah came forward, reached out, and took the scroll from his hand. When Uriah's fingers lightly brushed against his, David retracted his hand

and glared into the Hittite's eyes. What he saw there gave his heart a jolt. An expression of sorrow. And acceptance.

The man knew he was receiving his own death sentence.

Uriah tucked the small scroll inside his armor, against his heart. Then he turned and walked from the court with the bearing of a valorous soldier going out once again to prove his loyalty to the king.

+ + +

Bathsheba was unprepared for the news that came to her door. "Your husband, Uriah, has been killed in battle at Rabbah."

She stood gaping at the soldier standing before her. "What?"

"Your husband is dead."

"No. No!" As her legs buckled, her handmaiden embraced her. "Oh, my lady, my lady . . ." Bathsheba rocked back and forth, wailing and keening. Women came out of their houses up and down the street as Bathsheba sat in her doorway tearing the neckline of her dress and throwing dust upon her head as was the custom.

As the day wore on, other women were heard mourning their dead, but Bathsheba was too immersed in her own sorrow to wonder why so many grieved. Not until her mother came to her did suspicion sink its talons into her. For Bathsheba had not heard *all* the news from Rabbah, nor did she know of the rumors and gossip overflowing the king's court and palace, spilling into the streets of Jerusalem.

"Your cousin Miriam's husband is dead! And so is the husband of Havalah. Your husband, Uriah, was not the only man to die before the walls of Rabbah." She knelt in front of Bathsheba and glared at her. "Tell me what this means, Daughter. Tell me!"

Confused and frightened, Bathsheba drew back from the cynicism glittering in her mother's eyes. What was her mother implying? Why would these deaths have anything to do with her? "How would I know what happened in Rabbah, Mother?" Why was her mother blaming her for a battle that had happened miles from Jerusalem? It made no sense!

"Don't you know how people talk? Things done in the dark always come out into the light. Tell me about the message from the king, Bathsheba."

Bathsheba's alarm grew. "What message?"

"The one Joab received just before he sent men forward to the walls! And Joab didn't choose a weak spot where victory was certain. He chose a place where valiant Ammonites were positioned. They came out of the city and fought, and the servants of David fell." Her hand gripped Bathsheba's arm tightly. "Your father's cousin who serves the king thought David would cry out at the news of such needless loss of lives. But he didn't! Nor did he seem surprised by the news. Tell me why, Bathsheba!"

"*I don't know!*" Bathsheba gasped, face flushed. "Why should I know anything?" She tried to pull free, but her mother's fingers dug into her flesh. "Mother! You're hurting me!"

"Tell me, wretched girl! Why would a commander as wise in the ways of battle as Joab send men so close to the wall?" She gave Bathsheba a hard jerk. "Joab knows as well as everyone how King Abimelech, son of Gideon, was killed by a piece of millstone thrown down upon him by a woman on the wall. He even mentioned it in the message he sent to the king! There is no humiliation worse for a man than to be destroyed by a woman! Oh, my daughter, what have you done?"

Bathsheba felt the coldness in the pit of her stomach seep into her blood. "Nothing! I've done nothing!"

"Nothing!" Her mother sneered. "The messenger said, 'Uriah the Hittite was killed, too,' as though this was the news the king waited to hear!"

Bathsheba felt the blood drain from her face. "No," she choked. *"No!"* She shook her head, refusing to believe the accusation leveled against David. "They were friends," she stammered. "David would never . . ."

"David, is it? Do you know what *David* said about the news of your husband's death? He said to tell Joab not to be discouraged, for the sword kills one as well as another!" She spat the words bitterly, her face ravaged. "Your father is in Rabbah!"

"I didn't know this would happen! How could I know?"

Her mother let go of her and drew back. "So the rumors are true!" She looked ill and pinched with pain. "I threatened a woman who said she saw you being taken into the palace over a month ago. I prayed the rumors about you and the king were false. I told the woman not to repeat her lies. *Lies!* I should've known what you'd do if you ever had the chance!"

Crying, Bathsheba bent over, covering her head.

"Ohhh." Her mother moaned and rocked. "What have you done to us all? Ohhhhh . . ."

Gasping between her gulping sobs, Bathsheba confessed. "David saw me bathing from the roof of the palace. He sent for me. What could I do? He is the king!" Her mother slapped her hard across the face. Bathsheba recoiled, raising her arm to protect herself.

"And what did you do?" her mother spat. "Did you cover yourself? Did you call me for help? When he summoned you, did you do as Abigail did and tell him he would bring sin upon himself? You did none of those things! I can see the guilt written all over you, you wretched, stupid girl! *You harlot!* You've ruined us all!"

Bathsheba shook before her mother's fury. "I didn't mean to hurt anyone."

"I told you years ago David was not for you! I told you and told you! Why didn't you listen? *You've murdered your own husband!*"

"I didn't murder Uriah! *I didn't!* All I wanted was one night in the arms of the man I love, the man I've *always* loved. You knew! Did you try to help me? You always knew! I didn't mean for anyone to be hurt!"

"And you think *love* makes what you've done forgivable? Men fought with Uriah near the walls of Rabbah! Men died because of what you want!" She struck Bathsheba again, sobbing with anguish and rage. "You've brought shame upon my household! Shame upon your father! Shame upon Ahithophel! Do you think they'll ever forgive you? It would be better for me had I died in childbirth than to have given life to such as you! Disobedient daughter! Better had you been born dead!"

Bathsheba blocked another blow. "I carry David's child!"

Her mother uttered a broken sob and sank to her knees. "Ohhhh . . ." She wailed, her hands clenched over her ears. "Ohhhh . . ."

Bathsheba sobbed. "I didn't mean for this to happen, Mother! You have to believe me!"

"What does it matter what I believe? Fool! How many have died because of you? It will all be on your head. Do you think others won't learn of what the king has done for your sake? There are widows all over the city now who will curse you, and the king, too. And do you think the sons left fatherless today will rise up to praise David's name? Do you think they will take up arms for him? They will hate him with every breath they take! They will seek his destruction. And what of the thirty mighty men who fought with Uriah on David's behalf? What of your own father and all the others who've stood by David during his years in the wilderness? What will they think of their king now? Is he worthy of their loyalty and their life's blood? What will your father and grandfather do when they learn David murdered Uriah to have you? You are their flesh and blood, and you've betrayed them. They will never look at you again. People will spit on the ground when you pass by. They will never speak your name aloud! They will curse the day of your birth! And they will seek revenge upon the man who has ruined the reputation of their household!" Her mother tore the neckline of her dress as in mourning. "You are dead to me, dead to us all!"

Horrified, Bathsheba stretched out her hands, weeping and pleading. Her mother slapped her hands away and stood. Bathsheba rose to her knees and grasped her mother's dress. "Mother, please! Speak reason to them!"

Her mother shoved her away. "Reason? *You* dare speak of reason?" She kicked her.

Afraid for the child, Bathsheba cowered and curled into a ball, but her mother didn't strike her again. "You are cursed among women! Your name will be a byword for *adulteress!* Your name will be unspoken as long as I live!" She spit on her and went to the doorway. She stood there, her back to Bathsheba. "May the Lord God of Israel strike me down if your name ever crosses my lips again! May God do to you what you have done to others!" She fled into the street, leaving the door ajar behind her.

Scrambling over to it, Bathsheba closed and locked it.

Over the days that passed, she grieved the loss of her husband, the loss of the others who fought beside him, the loss of her family, the loss of her reputation as well as that of the king she still loved so desperately. She grieved over the chaos she knew would come because of her sin with the king and the murder of her husband. She fasted and wept for Uriah, collecting her tears in a small bottle she wore around her neck. She covered her head with ashes.

The formal mourning period of seven days ended, but the sorrow and shame would not lift. Her fears deepened, withering her soul. During the dark hours of night, Bathsheba understood why purity was so highly praised. She was paying the cost of disobedience now, and the price was higher than she ever could have imagined. One night of passion would cost her a lifetime of despair.

And the cost to others . . .

Soldiers entered her house eight days after Bathsheba had received the news of her husband's death. "We are under orders to bring the wife of Uriah the Hittite to the palace."

The wife of Uriah.

Bathsheba clutched against her heart the bottle filled with her tears.

The captain of the guard stepped forward. "You must come." Bathsheba left her house with nothing. She walked down the middle of the street with six soldiers as her escort. She wondered if David was showing her honor or merely protecting her. Women came to their doorways to watch the procession. One spit in the dust as she passed by. It seemed the eyes of Jerusalem were upon her—eyes of suspicion, eyes of hatred. She heard people whispering.

The guards didn't take her through a side entrance this time. They escorted her through the main entrance of the palace. The king was taking to wife the widow of one of his fallen mighty men. Perhaps it was meant as a show of great magnitude, for she was, after all, only a common woman, the daughter of a warrior, the granddaughter of a military adviser.

No one was fooled.

Except, perhaps, the king.

four

DAVID eagerly awaited the arrival of his newest wife. When the knock came upon his door, he opened it himself. Joram stood before him. He stepped aside and David saw a figure in black, head bowed. His pulse was racing. "The wife of Uriah the Hittite, my lord the king," Joram said smoothly.

David's head came up sharply. "Do not refer to her in that way again." He jerked his head in dismissal. He wanted no reminder that she'd belonged to another man before him. She belonged to *him* now. Nothing else mattered. As Joram's footsteps receded, David calmed himself.

"Bathsheba." His voice came out rough. She stood with eyes downcast like a shy virgin. "Ah, my love," he whispered. He took her hand. "I've missed you." She shivered slightly as she stepped hesitantly over the threshold. Her fingers were cold. Was she trembling with the same need he felt? He drew her into his bedchamber. "You've no need to be afraid anymore." He closed the door behind her. "You're with me now and always will be. Our child will be born with no cloud over him."

She said nothing.

Disturbed by her silence, David turned her to face him and tipped her chin. Her face was thinner, and she was as pale as alabaster. He removed the veil, and jealousy gripped him as he saw the small bottle on a string. He lifted it mockingly. "Did you love him so much?"

"I loved Uriah," she said softly. She raised her head. Her eyes were dark with pain. "But not as I've loved you. You were always the man of my dreams." She held out her free hand, palm up. "The man who held my heart in the palm of his hand." She clenched her fist, her eyes filling with tears.

David touched her cheek, marveling at the softness of her skin. She was the most beautiful woman in his kingdom, and she belonged to him now. "You'll never know how much I love you, Bathsheba." He saw her shudder and cupped her face. "You are *my* wife now." Ignoring the distressed look in her eyes, he removed the bottle of tears and tossed it aside. "Forget him. I will treat you like a queen." He leaned down and kissed her, gently at first, until he felt her respond. "All other women pale when compared to you." He dug his fingers into her hair.

✦　✦　✦

David stood just outside his door and read the note Joram had brought from one of his advisers. Matters of state beckoned. He crumpled the message impatiently. He didn't need to be reminded that he was responsible for the lives of his people, and it was time to return to matters of state. Joram waited, silent, eyes straight ahead.

"Summon the eunuch in charge of my harem," David said quietly so that Bathsheba wouldn't be disturbed from her sleep.

"Yes, my lord the king."

David went back into his bedchamber and closed the door quietly behind him.

He crossed the room and stood beside the bed, looking down at his wife. She was exquisite. He'd never seen a more beautiful woman, and he knew she would always be so. Like Abraham's Sarah. He smiled, taking a tress of black hair and rubbing it between his fingers. It was like thick silk. He would no longer be tormented by her absence. She belonged to him now. He could summon her any time he pleased.

Smiling, he sat on the edge of the bed. Leaning down, he kissed her and watched her awaken. She stretched and sighed softly. When she looked up at him, he realized she no longer had the look of starry-eyed adoration that she'd had as a young girl. Her love was mixed with troubled awareness. He didn't ask why. She reached up and touched his brow. He took her hand and pressed a kiss into her palm. "I don't want to leave you, but I must."

"You are the king."

"A chamber has been prepared for you." He stroked a tendril of curling black hair back from her brow. "If there is anything you need or want, you've only to tell the master of the harem. He will see to it."

A blush spread across her cheeks. He saw the moisture building in her eyes.

Stricken with emotions he couldn't identify, he grew impatient. "Up, my love." He had no time for teary brides! "We can't spend the rest of our lives in bed." He rose and moved away. The covers rustled behind him and he glanced back, intending to enjoy the pleasure of watching her dress. She reached for her widow's garb. *"No!"* He wrenched the garments from her, rolled them into a ball, and flung them into the corner. Shaken by the power of his emotions, he glared at her.

"Am I to enter your harem naked, my lord the king?"

He strode across the room and grabbed one of his own tunics. "Wear this!" He thrust it into her hands. She trembled violently as she put it on. The purple hem pooled around her feet. She looked so young and vulnerable; he was reminded of the little girl who'd followed him to the stream of En-gedi. "Bathsheba, I'm sorry."

A knocked sounded on the door, startling them both. He knew the eunuch had arrived to take her to her quarters. "Come!" he called out and the door opened. Bathsheba looked at the servant, but didn't take a step toward him. "I will call for you again soon," David said pointedly. Why should he feel guilty? Didn't she understand he was a king?

Her eyes flickered. Her cheeks filled with color as she bowed low. "I am yours to command, my lord the king." When she straightened, he saw a tear slip down her cheek before she turned quickly away. She followed the eunuch from the room.

David rubbed his chest, wondering why his heart should

ache so much when everything had turned out exactly as he'd planned.

+   +   +

Bathsheba's quarters were sumptuous, her new life one of leisure and luxury. She had beautiful clothing, plenty to eat, and the protection of the king. She was never alone, for more than two hundred people lived in David's palace—six of his other wives, their numerous handmaidens, his children, servants, secretaries, craftsmen, laborers, nannies, caretakers, cooks, guards, porters, stewards, and artisans. There were also many faithful elderly retainers and old soldiers who could no longer carry arms. A stream of visitors came and went into the palace as David's wives visited with their family members and entertained.

No one came to visit Bathsheba.

When David's wives gathered for the evening meal, they did not include her in their conversation, nor even acknowledge her presence. His older sons did look at her—pointedly: Amnon, the eldest, with lasciviousness; Absalom, with contempt. These women and their children were her family now, and Ahinoam had spoken for most of them the day Bathsheba had been shown into the women's quarter: "So this is the king's whore!"

She remembered overhearing her grandfather say to her father years ago, "Never trust anyone outside your own family." But Bathsheba knew she could never trust any of these women or their sons, and her child would always be in danger.

The days wore on her like a windstorm over stone. Whispered words blew harsh, rubbing painfully, reshaping her.

Bathsheba sat alone, consoling herself with love for the child she carried. When her son came, she wouldn't give him up to a wet nurse or a nanny. She would keep him with her and love him. And if the child was a girl, she would watch over her and train her into womanhood herself, rather than entrust her to the care of others. And she hoped. *Let the child be a son to make David proud!*

She waited a month before letting the news be known that she was carrying the king's child. There were some in the palace whose loyalty toward David ran so deep they refused to think ill of him, no matter what others whispered. They rejoiced that the king's household was about to grow by another child. However, there were many who cast sidelong glances at her, lips sneering. Some would not look at her at all.

The wives spent every day entertaining themselves with games, music, conversation. Some did handwork to while away the hours. Whenever word came that the king would spend the evening with them, they focused all their energies on preparing for his visitation. Each tried to outdo the others in beauty preparation. They primped and fussed, sending handmaidens hither and yon for whatever they thought might attract David's attention. Ahinoam put on Egyptian kohl and Persian mascara. Maacah painted her toenails with henna and wore anklets. They all braided their hair and anointed themselves with perfume. Bathsheba bathed, brushed her hair until it shone and rippled over her shoulders and down her back, and wore the simple dress of a commoner. Let David remember her as she had been, not as she had become.

When David entered the room, her heart leaped. She watched as he looked around. His gaze settled briefly upon her and his eyes glowed warmly. But he looked away, speaking to Ahinoam, who caressed his arm and smiled up at him as though he were the moon and the stars. Though he did not linger long, David wandered the room, pausing here and there, giving each a measure of attention.

Bathsheba observed his every movement with increasing anguish. He greeted each woman with a smile, talked amicably, charmed them with a touch. He was so handsome, who would not love him? She felt a shaft of pain each time he brushed his knuckles against an upturned face, took a hand and kissed it, spoke a soft word, or laughed. The women flirted boldly, some so boldly Bathsheba wanted to scream and tear their hair out. But she remained in her seat, pretending a calm she didn't feel. When David sat upon a cushion, he was surrounded and caressed. He looked at her only one more time, but she took little comfort in the darkening of his eyes, for his attention was drawn away almost immediately.

So this was the pain her mother had warned her against! Hadn't her mother tried to tell her what it would be like to be David's wife? *"One among many."* Could there be any agony worse than seeing the man she loved pampered and petted by six other women? She shifted her body so that she wouldn't have to endure it.

David came to her then. "Are you well, Bathsheba?" She was too distressed to answer, afraid if she spoke she would give the women fuel for further torment when David was gone. "Bathsheba?" He spoke in a hoarse whisper and hunkered down as he turned her face so that she had to look at him. He searched her eyes, his own hungry and troubled. "Try to understand. I can't give in to what I want and forsake all these others."

The irony of his words made her look away. Hadn't she forsaken all others for him? Wasn't her husband now dead because she had given in to what she wanted without thought of the consequences?

"Bathsheba," he said again, her name a soft groan. The others watched like a pride of lionesses.

"Of course I understand," she whispered, looking into his eyes and hoping he didn't sense her despair. Understanding increased her suffering. He was a king, above all. And a king must have many wives so he could build up his house with sons. Now that it was known that she was already with child, what need had he to call her to his bed? She remembered her mother's words. *"When you grow up, you will understand the wisdom of worshiping God and not a man."*

She must grow up and throw away her fantasies! She must face her circumstances! There would be worse scandal if the king summoned her now that her pregnancy was known. Everyone knew the only reason the king visited a wife was to beget more children. She and David couldn't be alone together until after the child was born and she'd fulfilled the rites of purification—forty days for a boy, eighty for a girl. *Oh, let it be a boy!*

Her heart sank as she thought about the months of loneliness ahead of her. For she was despised among these women, the object of their jealousy, the victim of their constant gossip. But what right had she to resent them? Everything they said was true!

David brushed his fingers against her cheek and rose. With a heavy heart, she watched him walk away. Bowing her head, she took up her embroidery and kept her gaze away from him for the rest of the evening. Her heart fluttered and her forehead broke out in a cold sweat. She knew exactly how long he spoke with each wife. Never had she thought her sweet dreams of David could turn into such a nightmare! She was torn between relief and dread when the king finally rose to leave the company of his wives. She knew when he looked at her, but she didn't look up. She kept thinking of how he'd sung to his men around the fire, looking from one to the next. She was no more or less regarded by the king than any other woman in this room. She was just one of many who lived to be in his company. Her mother had told her so time and again, but life was her teacher.

The women relaxed as soon as the doors were closed behind the king. They no longer competed for his attention. Some talked. Some lounged indolently. Others returned to their handwork. When the eunuch entered the chamber, they fell silent. "Abigail," he said, and she rose quickly, cheeks flushed as she followed him out of the room.

Never had Bathsheba felt such pain! Her heart felt as though it were being torn from her! Maacah smirked. Haggith whispered behind her hand to Eglah, who laughed and looked across the room at Bathsheba. Did her anguish show? She wanted to leap up and run. She wanted to lock herself in her private chamber and scream out her pain.

Ahinoam sniffed. "Why is he calling for Abigail? He hasn't called for her in months. Besides, she's too old to bear him another son."

"Better her than another whose name I won't mention."

Maacah glared at Bathsheba. "Perhaps David craves the company of a *virtuous* woman."

Words of retaliation rose like bile in Bathsheba's throat, but she swallowed them. Why pour oil on the fire? Besides, what defense had she? She *was* faithless. She gathered her sewing, rose, inclined her head, and walked sedately from the room, refusing to give them further opportunities to stab her heart. When her chamber door was firmly closed, she crumpled to the floor and stifled her sobs with a pillow.

She slept little that night, tortured by thoughts of David and Abigail. She rose early and walked alone in the inner garden. She sat beneath an olive tree and bowed her head, afraid to pray. Why draw God's attention when the price for sin was death? She moved her hands slowly over her abdomen, love distracting her from her anguish. She would pour her life out for her child. David's child.

"Bathsheba?"

Startled, she glanced at Abigail.

"I've come from the king," the older woman said.

Bathsheba's heart twisted. She clenched her hands in her lap, her stomach tightening. Did Abigail mean to gloat over the night she'd spent in David's arms? With an effort, Bathsheba kept silent, refusing to show her feelings.

David's third wife studied her for a moment. "May I sit?"

"If it pleases you."

Abigail took a seat beside her. "I'm not here to cause you

more sorrow, Bathsheba." She looked down and brushed imaginary dust from her dress. "David asked me last night if you are adjusting to life in the palace. I told him you've shown great dignity. He asked if you've been well, and I told him I haven't heard you utter a word of complaint. He asked if you've received visitors, and I said not to my knowledge." She gave a soft broken laugh. "I suppose our husband felt he could speak with me about these things because I'm older than he and was married to another before him. I suppose he thought I would understand your feelings better than anyone else in the palace." She drew in her breath and released it slowly. "He also asked me if you still grieved for Uriah."

Fighting tears, Bathsheba stared straight ahead.

Abigail lifted her head and turned to look at her. "I've never known David to ask so many questions about a wife, or to show jealousy over one. He's always been very careful to treat each one equally to preserve peace in the household. We all vie for his attention, but he has never before found distinction among us. Last night, he let his heart be known. Not because he wanted everyone to know, but because he can't help himself. He has a special regard for you."

Bathsheba sucked in a sharp breath as joy caught her off guard. She quickly dampened it when she recognized the pain in Abigail's eyes. How many others were in love with him? "I'm sorry, Abigail."

Abigail understood her meaning and smiled wryly. "It is never wise to fall in love with a king."

"My mother told me that years ago."

"Your mother is wise." She lifted her eyes. "I think David is in love with you. I don't think he could've done the things he's done otherwise."

Heat surged into Bathsheba's cheeks, but strangely she heard no condemnation in Abigail's tone, nor saw it in her eyes. She trembled. "I'm the one who sinned." It was better for all if she took full responsibility.

Abigail shook her head. "We've all sinned."

"*You* didn't. You warned David against sinning." She didn't have to add the rest—that she'd unwittingly encouraged him to do so.

"I called my husband a fool before witnesses."

"You remained faithful."

"And waited until Nabal was sober so that I could tell him what he had done and have him understand completely. I knew his greed. I knew his arrogance. I also knew his cowardice. I spoke and watched the terror come upon him. I watched him die, and thanked God for my deliverance. And when David sent for me to be his wife, I packed in all haste and came to him because I'd loved what I'd heard about him and loved him still more when I laid eyes upon him." Her eyes were shiny with tears. "I love him still."

Bathsheba was deeply touched that Abigail trusted her enough to be so open. "You did nothing deserving of condemnation. Everyone spoke of your wisdom and quick actions. You saved countless lives that night, Abigail." Whereas Uriah was dead because of her, as were all the men who had stormed the walls of Rabbah with him.

"Do not praise me. God sees the heart, Bathsheba, and God will judge us all."

Bathsheba felt a chill in the pit of her stomach. Closing her eyes, she hung her head. "That's what I fear most of all." *I've broken the Law. How can I ever undo what has happened because of my sin? Oh, Lord God of Israel, be merciful. Please pull me up from the pit I dug for myself and change the direction of my life!*

Abigail put her hand over hers and squeezed it gently. "God is also merciful to those who repent." She rose, leaving Bathsheba alone to wonder how repentance would change anything now. No matter what she did from here forward, people would remember her as an adulteress.

The child she carried would be the evidence held against her.

✦   ✦   ✦

When the child came, Bathsheba saw in the eyes of those who assisted her that her sins were now revealed. The eighth wife of the king, a mere six months after entering the palace, had born a fully developed child with strong limbs and lungs. As her baby screamed in the midwife's arms, Bathsheba felt the woman's repugnance. She looked from face to face and was afraid. Ignoring the pain and summoning her strength, she reached out quickly. "Give me my son!"

The midwife dumped him into her arms as though he were an unclean thing. Shocked by such careless handling, Bathsheba drew back from the woman and held her son close. If she'd ever wondered what treatment her child would receive, she knew now. The entire population of the palace—nay, the nation—would know her son had been conceived in sin!

The birth attendants left, but Bathsheba heard their voices buzz just outside her door.

Abigail entered soon afterward. "Would you mind if I stayed with you for a while?"

Bathsheba wept at her kindness. "I understand their hatred of me, but my son is *innocent!*"

Abigail brushed the hair back from her face. "Hush now, for the child's sake." She tucked her hands beneath the infant. "Let me have him. I'll wash him and rub the salt in gently so he'll be safe from infection. Then I'll swaddle him and present him to the king."

Where her grandfather, Ahithophel, would see and know . . .

David had offered him many gifts upon his return from Rabbah. David assured her that all was well between them, but she knew David would be dead by now if he were not king. Her grandfather was shrewd, but he was also as unforgiving as Joab. She feared what went on in the mind of her grandfather. When David had returned at the head of his army with Hanun's crown upon his head, she'd watched her grandfather from the palace wall as he came into the city at the head of the military advisers. He looked up and saw her where she stood. He didn't smile and raise his hand. His eyes fixed upon her like a target.

Bathsheba could only hope her father hadn't been told the whole story when he'd been transported home after being wounded in Rabbah. Had her mother taken pity upon her as her father lay suffering? Surely she would not have been so cruel as to tell him his daughter had committed adultery with the king and caused the murder of her husband! It would have been an act of kindness to tell him simply that his daughter had been taken into the palace as the king's wife after news of Uriah's death—and omit the rest of the sordid tale.

She had frequent nightmares, awakening in a cold sweat and expecting to see her grandfather leaning over her with his curved knife. Sometimes she dreamed she was standing at the door of her father's house, hearing her grandfather swear to his son in her hearing, "Oh, my son, my son! They will not go unpunished! Though David be king, I will lay him low! And if I meet failure, may my life be forfeit!"

She tried not to think of what the future might hold. She tried to forget the bad dreams and separation from David as she held son in her arms and nursed him. Perhaps this would be enough.

David was pleased with her son. He sat with her and cupped the child's head tenderly, then looked into her eyes. She decided to live for each infrequent moment in David's company, basking in his love, even if it proved inconstant. Her son would be different. She relished his warmth in her arms, the tug of his mouth at her breast as he took his sustenance from her. Never had she loved anyone as much as she loved this child of her body. She dedicated herself to him. Night and day, she watched over him, entrusting his care to no one else. She kept him close, aware of his every movement and sound. A child existed to be loved, and she poured her love out like an offering upon him.

And then the prophet Nathan came to set things right.

✦   ✦   ✦

David was informed the moment Nathan approached the palace, and he came into the court to offer the elderly man warm welcome and greeting. He tensed when he saw the fire in the old prophet's eyes and realized that Nathan had come with less than pleasant words to impart. "What brings you to the palace?" David said, taking his seat and resting his hands on the arms of the throne. "What can I do for you?"

Nathan stood before him, feet planted. He was far older than David's forty years, but life shone brightly in his eyes. The presence of the Lord could be felt in the room the moment he opened his mouth and spoke in a deep, clear voice for all to hear.

"There were two men in a certain town. One was rich, and one was poor. The rich man owned many sheep and cattle. The poor man owned nothing but a little lamb he had worked hard to buy. He raised that little lamb, and it grew up with his children. It ate from the man's own plate and drank from his cup. He cuddled it in his arms like a baby daughter. One day a guest arrived at the home of the rich man. But instead of killing a lamb from his own flocks for food, he took the poor man's lamb and killed it and served it to his guest."

David slammed his fist upon the arm of his throne. "As surely as the Lord lives, any man who would do such a thing deserves to die! He must repay four lambs to the poor man for the one he stole and for having no pity."

Nathan's eyes blazed. "*You are that man!*"

David went cold, his skin prickling.

Nathan stepped forward. "The Lord, the God of Israel says," he said in a voice all the more powerful because of its quietness, "'I anointed you king of Israel and saved you from the power of Saul. I gave you his house and his wives and the kingdoms of Israel and Judah. And if that had not been enough, I would have given you much, much more.'"

Fear gripped David until he shook.

"'Why, then, have you despised the word of the Lord and done this horrible deed? For you have murdered Uriah and stolen his wife.'"

All those in the court gasped and stared at David. Drops of sweat formed on his brow and dripped down his temples. His ears were opened! For he heard the truth Nathan spoke. His eyes were opened fully to the evil he'd done, and he cried out in horror. How could he have been so blind? How was it possible to love God so much and be captured so completely by sin? David bolted out of his throne and threw himself to his knees at the feet of the prophet, his heart thundering as he felt the eyes of God upon him.

"'From this time on,'" Nathan went on, "'the sword will be a constant threat to your family, because you have despised Me by taking Uriah's wife to be your own. Because of what you have done, I, the Lord, will cause your own household to rebel against you. I will give your wives to another man, and he will go to bed with them in public view. You did it secretly, but I will do this to you openly in the sight of all Israel.'"

Sorrow filled David. "I have sinned against the Lord!" He deserved death. He remembered the look in Uriah's eyes before he turned away and went to face his death. *How could I have done it?* David wept. *My friend! My friend!* He waited for God to strike him down.

Instead, he felt Nathan's hand gentle upon his head. "Yes, but the Lord has forgiven you, and you won't die for this sin."

David's head came up in amazement. Nathan stroked his hair as though he were a child, his eyes grieved. "But," he said sadly, straightening, "you have given the enemies of the Lord great opportunity to despise and blaspheme Him, so your child will die."

David's stomach dropped. He stared into Nathan's eyes and saw there would be no compromise. His chest tightened as he thought of the cost to Bathsheba. Shutting his eyes, he bent over and covered his head as Nathan turned and walked from the court.

✦   ✦   ✦

Bathsheba was alarmed when her baby wouldn't nurse, then frightened when he became feverish and cried pitifully. She did everything she knew to bring the fever down, but it raged unabated, sapping the child of strength. She held him and rocked him. She walked with him in her arms. When she became too exhausted to hold him, she lay upon her bed with the baby nestled against her. And she wept, hour upon unending hour, for fear of losing him.

"Where is David? Does he know . . . ?"

"He knows, my lady," the eunuch told her. "He's fasting and inquiring of God for the child."

Bathsheba felt a flicker of hope at this news, for hadn't the Lord always heard David's prayers? Hadn't God always helped David?

She didn't dare beseech God herself.

Each day, the child lost strength. On the seventh day, while Bathsheba was holding him and pleading softly, the baby stopped breathing. For a long moment, Bathsheba felt as though her own heart had stopped. She didn't cry out or tear her hair or rent her clothing. She lay quietly upon her bed and curled her body around her dead child, and closed her eyes.

God, I know you've taken my son. Why didn't you take me instead?

Some of the women who'd lost children pitied her. But others took cruel pleasure in God's judgment upon Bathsheba's baby and her anguished silence. "She deserved it," they whispered. "See what God does to sinners!" they gossiped. "She's getting a taste of the bitterness she's caused others."

Abigail sat with Bathsheba, weeping and stroking her hair, but saying nothing. The older woman simply held her as the little body was taken from her. Bathsheba wept hysterically.

Finally, exhausted and heartsick, Bathsheba lay staring at nothing. "David never came. Not once. I sent word. He knew our child was dying. And he never came. I thought he loved us."

Abigail put her hand on Bathsheba's shoulder. "He's been fasting and praying for seven days. He beseeched God's mercy continuously, Bathsheba. The priests were afraid to tell him that your baby has died. They thought he might kill himself."

Bathsheba sat up, frightened.

Abigail shook her head quickly. "Don't be alarmed. I was told David already knew what had happened when the men came to speak with him. He arose from the ground, washed, anointed himself, changed his clothes, and went into the house of the Lord to worship. He returned to the palace and is taking a meal."

Bathsheba sank down again and turned her face away. "God is so cruel."

"You mustn't say that."

"Why shouldn't I say it? He should've struck *me* down instead of killing an innocent child! Let God strike me now!" She pulled her hair, her chest heaving with the rising sobs. "It was *my* sin—*mine!* Why take out His wrath on a helpless baby?" She gulped breath as she cried. "My son . . . oh, my son . . ."

Abigail cupped Bathsheba's cheek. "You'll become sick if you go on like this."

"Let me be sick unto death!" Weeping, Bathsheba drew her knees into her chest and covered her head. "Why did God let my son suffer for my sins? Why?"

"I don't know," Abigail said.

Desolate, Bathsheba turned her face to the wall and said no more.

+ + +

David's advisers were quick to give their opinion, speaking to him hurriedly as he finished his meal. "It would be wise, my lord the king, to establish separate quarters for the wife of Uriah. You must see no more of her."

David raised his head, seeing the way the wind blew. It was always easier to attack the weak.

"The people," another said. "You must think of the people."

He *was* thinking of his people. The impact of his sin upon them weighed heavily on his mind and heart. How could he have been so blind? How could he have done the things he did without seeing the evil in it? The men surrounded him like old hens, looking for someone to peck to pieces.

"Of course, you must assign guards to protect the woman from those who will want to take justice into their own hands."

"Cloister her as you have cloistered Michal."

"It might serve you better if you sent the woman to live in Hebron or Jericho."

David shoved his plate away and stood. "I've listened to your advice." He glared at his advisers. "Bathsheba will not be punished for sins I committed. I confessed before God and repented. And I will make the truth known to the people."

Those who loved him quickly capitulated, but there were others who merely bowed their heads and pretended obedience. David knew them well. Hadn't he spent years in the desert with these men? Fine clothes and houses hadn't changed them. There would always be those inside the palace who crouched like hungry lions, seeking an opportunity to devour their prey.

"Nathan said God has forgiven me for my sins."

"Yes, my lord the king. The Lord has forgiven *you*. God said nothing in regard to the woman."

The woman. Amazing how two words could convey such contempt. "Bathsheba is innocent of Uriah's death."

"Is a woman ever innocent, my lord the king? Was it not the woman in the Garden of Eden who drew the man into sin?"

He looked into their eyes and was chilled by their lack of mercy. How quick they were to absolve him because he sat upon the throne but pour blame for everything upon a defenseless woman.

"You are beloved by all Israel," one said, but David knew his flattering tongue was dipped in poison.

"I was the shepherd who led the lamb astray."

"You are king, and the nation is at stake, my lord. Isn't it an unblemished lamb that is offered as atonement for sin?"

David's eyes filled with tears at the hardness of their hearts. "The Lord chose the lamb. He took our son." He turned his back on them and went straight to the women's quarters. He had neglected Bathsheba for too long, serving these men who devised evil plans against her.

His heart broke when he entered her room and saw her curled on her side facing the wall. He dismissed her hand-maiden with a nod of his head and sat on the edge of the bed. "Bathsheba." Her body jerked and she covered her head with her arms. "Bathsheba." He turned her and pulled her into his arms. "I'm sorry."

"Our son . . . our son . . ." She clung to him, sobbing, her fingers clutching at his tunic.

David pressed his face into the curve of her neck and wept with her. "The sin is upon my head," he said hoarsely.

She pulled away from him violently, her face ravaged by grief. "No, no. It was me."

"Bathsheba . . ."

"Who was it who followed you around the camp? Who was it who could look only at you when her groom sat beside her? Who was it who stood naked in her courtyard so that you could see her? Who was it who went into your arms without a thought for her husband?" She beat her fists against her heart. "Me! It was me!"

David caught hold of her wrists. "God didn't punish our son, Bathsheba. He took him out of the reach of evil men." Like those he had just left. Like others within his own house who would use this to rise against him. "How many would've used the circumstances of our son's birth to blaspheme against God? The Lord has kept our son from harm."

"I want my son! I want to hold my son!"

David gripped her head and looked into her red-rimmed, tear-drenched eyes. "He's in the Lord's hands, my love. I can't bring him back to you." He pulled her close again, rocking her as though she were a child in need of comfort. "Someday we will go and be with him."

Bathsheba relaxed against him. "The Lord must hate me."

"No." He tenderly combed the dark lank hair back from her face. His heart squeezed tight at the pallor of her cheeks, the suffering in her eyes. "I misused my authority, Bathsheba. When I saw you, I asked who you were. Did I have a thought for your husband or your father or grandfather? I remembered the little girl who had followed me about the camp with her heart in her eyes. I saw the beautiful woman you'd become, and I wanted you. Nothing mattered but to satisfy my own lust. I gave no thought of the cost to others, especially the cost to you."

FRANCINE RIVERS

"I should've been like Abigail, warning you . . ."

"I was a different man when Abigail confronted me, Bathsheba. Young and on fire for the Lord. I was running for my life in those days. Look around you. You see the way I live now. When I saw you from the roof, I was a king blinded by pride." Pain filled him as he saw himself clearly now. He had shirked his duty as commander of the army. He'd grown bored and restless while living his life of leisure in the palace. When he saw a woman of unusual beauty bathing, he sent soldiers to bring her to him. Why shouldn't he take whatever he wanted? He was *king!*

What a fool he'd been.

"I was so conceited! I thought I held all power in my hand. I thought I could have whatever I wanted. So I stole you from another, sired a child, then tried to use my friend to hide the evidence of my sin. Uriah proved himself more righteous than I." He felt her shudder in his arms.

"He knew," she said softly.

"Yes, he knew." He shut his eyes, stricken again. "The judgment is on my head, Bathsheba, because I shed innocent blood." He was filled with self-loathing and grief. "After all the Lord has done for me, I allowed lust to control me and turned away from the One who had given me victory on every side."

"I share the blame. I used love as an excuse to sin."

"You didn't kill Uriah."

"A man's heart can die before a spear ever pierces him." Tears streamed down her pale cheeks. Uriah had been a good husband, an honest man, and she'd crushed his heart and been the motive behind his murder.

David pressed her head against his heart, unable to speak. How was it possible for two people to know and love the Law and yet sin so abominably? How and when had sin first crept into their lives and spread like a plague until it killed their consciences? Had the seeds of sin been planted years ago, when he'd realized she was no longer a child and wished he had asked for her before Eliam gave her to another man? Had the seeds planted then been watered with his own fantasies?

Yet, what he felt for Bathsheba wasn't lust. Not entirely. He *loved* her.

Tipping her chin, David kissed her. Her lips trembled, and he sensed her hesitance. He kissed her again and felt her respond. When he lifted his head, she leaned against him again with a soft sigh. "God has forgiven us," he said, closing his eyes and giving silent thanks. "The Lord has shown His great mercy in giving us our lives. And He did *not* say I had to give you up."

"But how shall we live, knowing what we've done and the harm it's brought to others?"

"We will live one day at a time and face whatever comes."

"It'll never be over. Oh, David, I see so clearly now, and it hurts so much. We won't be the only ones to suffer." She drew back, looking up at him. "If only we were the only ones . . ."

He cupped her cheek. "Nathan proclaimed the word of the Lord. I know what is to come."

She went into his arms and clung fiercely. "I love you,

David. I've always loved you. No matter what happens, I always will."

"I know," he said with a sad smile.

Love was never the issue between the two of them. He loved her too, more fiercely than he had ever loved a woman. But he was deeply grieved when he remembered the loyal friends he'd betrayed because he thought his love for Bathsheba provided adequate excuse: Uriah, who had fought beside him in more battles than he could remember; Eliam, who'd shared his fire and food; Ahithophel, his brilliant military adviser. Would they still stand with him? Love betrayed turned to hate. Now, Ahithophel never spoke Bathsheba's name; her mother hadn't attended her during the birth of her child. Bathsheba had been abandoned by her family, though she hadn't once complained.

David vowed silently to do all he could to mend the broken relationships, to renew trust, and to glorify God's name.

"I'm sorry," he said, heartbroken at the pain he had caused her. He prayed that the honor he showed her as the woman he loved would eventually soften the hearts of those he'd hurt and humiliated.

"Our son." Her body shook violently as she began weeping again. "Our son . . ."

David gathered his young wife into his arms and comforted her the only way he knew how. And as he did, he prayed that God would show them even more mercy by granting them another child to replace the one who had paid the price for their sin.

WHEN Bathsheba realized she was with child again, she was afraid to rejoice. Would God take this child also? Would she have another baby, only to have it die in her arms like her firstborn son?

Cloistered in luxury, favored wife of an absent king, she lived a life of sorrow and loneliness, shunned by family and friends. David was in Rabbah with the army, leaving her vulnerable and unprotected from the enemies that surrounded her. People outside the walls judged her a harlot and condemned her, just as her mother had. How could she hope for God's mercy when her own mother hated her? How could she believe God had forgiven her sins when no one else had? The prophet Nathan told David that God had forgiven him, but did that forgiveness extend to her as well? David had claimed so, but Bathsheba would make no assumptions. She lived in constant fear, for she had no possessions of her own, no money to buy sacrifices. All she had to offer God was a contrite heart and the desire to do right for the rest of her life.

How she longed to go back in time, to be a child again, safe in her mother's arms. How she longed to be on her grandfather's knee, listening to him dispense wisdom to those who came to visit at their fire. Once she had been an innocent girl full of unrequited love for a handsome warrior, a singer of psalms, the charismatic leader of a growing army. Now she was David's eighth wife, known far and wide as the adulteress who had enticed a beloved king into murdering her husband so she could live in the palace. The people forgave David, but used her as their scapegoat.

She did not resent the people's lenience with David. Someone had to bear the blame, and it was better laid upon her head than having the people turn on him. She was just a woman, but he was their king.

But, oh, how can I ever hold my head up again? When I sing praises to the Lord, people glare at me as though I'm blaspheming. They come to worship You and see me among the women, and their hearts are turned away from You as they nurture thoughts of vengeance.

Bathsheba begged God to blot out her transgressions, to cleanse her from all sin. "Give me a heart that will be pleasing to You, Lord. Don't cast me out into the darkness." But even as she prayed, she felt overwhelming shame at being so presumptuous. What right had she to ask for mercy?

Fear attacked most often at night when she was alone in

her chamber. What right had she to hold a baby in her arms? None! How many mothers wept over the loss of sons who had died with Uriah? How many wives grieved the death of husbands or brothers or cousins? She had no right to happiness.

But the child, oh, the child.

"Oh, God of mercy, only You can deliver me from my guilt. Oh, Lord, comfort those who mourn. Give them joy in the morning. Do with me whatever You will, but please spare my baby, who is innocent of the sins I committed."

With so many pointing fingers and shaking their heads, Bathsheba didn't hope for mercy.

The baby came easily, and her son was strong and healthy and beautiful. Bathsheba held her second son and wept. Overwhelmed with tenderness, yet still afraid, she gazed at her baby as he nursed. The fingers of his right hand clasped tightly around her thumb. "I promise to raise up my son to be a man after Your own heart. I will teach him to love Your Law." Tears streaked her face as she raised her son's tiny hand and kissed it. "And I give him the name Solomon, for it is through his birth that I have come to experience *God's peace*."

Please, please, let it be so between us, Lord. Forgive me.

A message came within a few hours, written by the hand of Nathan the prophet. "*Your son shall have the name Jedidiah—'beloved of the Lord.'*"

Bathsheba laughed. *Oh, Lord, You have washed me clean and warmed me in Your lovingkindness*. Even when all those around her scorned her and failed to celebrate the birth of her son, God looked with favor upon him and gave His blessing.

She was filled with amazement and gratitude. "My son . . . my son . . ." She wept with joy. She kissed his small face. "I took my troubles to the Lord. I, so unworthy, cried out to Him for deliverance, and He has answered from His throne." She laughed joyfully, tears of exultation dripping like a baptism upon Solomon's brow. She smoothed them over his soft skin. "Jedidiah." She kissed each cheek and nestled him against her shoulder. "Jedidiah." She savored the feel of his body tucked close. "My cup is overflowing with God's blessings," she whispered, rubbing his back.

Jedidiah. The Lord had named *her* son *"beloved of the Lord."*

✦   ✦   ✦

Rabbah fell, and the defeated Ammonites were set to work with saw, iron threshing boards, and iron axes, tearing down the temple and altars of the Ammonite god Molech and the walls of the city. Before leading his army away, David left orders for the Ammonites. When the demolition was done, they were to turn their work to the brick kilns and rebuild the conquered cities according to his specifications.

David led his army into Jerusalem, wearing the crown of Molech upon his head to show that false gods could not stand against the Lord. The people cheered as he rode through the gate, leading the way for wagons loaded with booty. His commanders and advisers followed, and the troops came marching home.

Bathsheba saw her grandfather among David's advisers

and hoped there would be peace between them. Perhaps
Ahithophel would forgive her when he learned he had a
great-grandson. Still, she was chilled by what she'd heard
from Joram. David had not gone to Rabbah on his own.
Joab had sent for him to come, for he'd won the battle and
the crown was waiting for David. Joab might as well have
said: *You are king and will wear the crown, but never forget
I am the one who conquered Rabbah!*

She was afraid for David.

Joab and his brother Abishai were both fierce warriors
given to quick insult and long-lasting thirst for vengeance.
Bathsheba remembered hearing in Uriah's home about
Joab's vengeful murder of Abner, one of the most powerful
men in King Saul's army. Abner had killed Joab's brother
Asahel just after the contest held at the pool of Gibeon. Joab
had then taken the life of Abner in revenge. Bathsheba
recalled hearing how furious David had been and how he
mourned Abner's death. She had been among the people
when David condemned Joab's actions as evil. At the time,
she had been afraid for David. And now Joab was even
more powerful, more evil.

Was it not Joab's idea to send other men with Uriah to
their deaths? Although attempting to cover David's orders
to murder Uriah, he'd added tenfold to the consequences of
David's sin. Even the message he'd sent to David after
Uriah's death was a challenge: He had reminded David that
Gideon's son Abimelech was killed by a piece of millstone
thrown down upon him by a woman on the wall. She knew
Joab had been pointing an accusing finger at her, predict-
ing that she would cause David's downfall.

Joab was a threat to David, even if David was unable—
or unwilling—to see it.

And how many other enemies were rising within David's
own ranks and within his own family? How many would
whisper lies and make secret plots to destroy him? How
many would set snares and lie in wait, devising schemes to
bring him down? Nathan had warned him.

The palace was fraught with tension and hostility,
rampant with jealousy and ambition. She saw how David's
other wives were bringing their sons up to be contenders
for the throne. They were hungry to grasp power for their
offspring. They saw David's love for her as a threat. David's
sons ran wild with pride and arrogance, and he did nothing
to dissuade them.

Bathsheba feared her grandfather most. She had grown up
among fighting men. She had listened to the conversations
around her grandfather Ahithophel's campfire. She had
listened to her father talk about enemies and allies. Was her
grandfather now pretending forgiveness while plotting
revenge? Could she believe that Ahithophel would forgive
and forget the humiliation she and David had brought upon
his house? Her grandfather was brilliant in the tactics of
warfare. He would know how to destroy a king.

When she spoke with David of her concerns, he dismissed
her fears. "I've spoken with Ahithophel at length. He swore
his allegiance to me. Besides, my love, I've given him gifts,
more than twice the bride-price of Ahinoam. So don't
worry yourself about things a woman can't possibly understand."

She understood that David had tried to show her grandfather that he valued her more than any other and would show her the honor of a first wife. But the gift could easily be seen as a bribe, and her grandfather had always been uncompromising. A man's hatred could run deeper than any gift could reach. But nothing she could say would convince David to be cautious when heeding the military advice of her grandfather. He refused to look upon Ahithophel as a possible enemy.

It was the first time she and David had argued, and the first time David left her bed before sunrise. Nor did he speak to her during the next visitation.

When Bathsheba learned that David had taken another wife, a girl several years younger than she and the daughter of a powerful merchant of the tribe of Benjamin, Bathsheba felt betrayed. Weeping, she went before the Lord and prayed. She spent hours thinking about her situation and finally realized she was being childish again. David was *king* and would never belong entirely to her. If she didn't accept her station in life as one of his many wives, she would make herself and him miserable.

David would take more wives and concubines in the years ahead. She would have to learn to live with the pain that would come each time his eyes drifted to another. When David's young bride was ushered into the women's quarters, Bathsheba mastered her jealousy and greeted her as she would have wished to be greeted.

In the midst of her suffering, Bathsheba grew up. She'd loved David since she was a little girl. She had placed him on a pedestal like an idol. But she knew now that David wasn't a god. He was an ordinary man who'd been made

extraordinary through the tender mercies of God. David
was a man capable of great victories, but also of horrendous
defeat. Hadn't his lust for her almost destroyed him? Her
weakness might yet destroy her. If David were to die, she
and her son would be at the mercy of men like her grandfather and Joab, or whichever of David's sons could wrestle
power from the hands of the others.

When fear threatened to overwhelm her, she set her mind
upon the Lord, comforting herself with thoughts of what
God had already done for her. She sang her husband's
psalms to her son—and clung to the promises in them. And
every time she did these things, she felt an inner peace. The
Lord was her shield, her deliverer, the lifter of her soul. Not
David. David was only the man she loved, not the God she
now worshiped.

Knowing her husband's faults and weaknesses didn't
diminish him in her sight. Strangely, she loved him all the
more because of his vulnerability. Two years of suffering
had awakened her. Power was in the hand of the Lord! And
so, she went down on her knees daily, bending her head to
the floor each morning when she first awakened so that she
could thank God for His blessings and ask for His guidance.
She prayed constantly that God would protect David and
give him wisdom. And whenever she was in David's
company, she did all she could to give comfort, pleasure,
and joy. She knew a contentious wife was worse than a
constant dripping and submitted herself to his needs, even
those he didn't realize he had—especially for someone to
listen to him.

She was no longer a child filled with dreams, but a

woman tempered by hardship and sorrow. She spoke often
with the prophet Nathan, seeking his wisdom because she
knew it would come from God. When she lay down at
night, whether in David's arms or alone in her private
chamber while he was in bed with another woman, she
praised God for all the day had held, both good and bad.

Every time David added another wife or concubine to his
harem, the hurt would rise in her again. But she learned not
to expect perfect love from David, for to have those expec-
tations increased her suffering. She refused to give in to the
emotions tearing at her heart and remembered the source of
love. She turned her attention from David's wandering eye
to God and His faithfulness to His people. Her husband
could still arouse her physical passion, and she could still
feel suffering, betrayal, confusion, and loneliness. But she
was no longer in despair, no longer without hope. The Lord
God of Israel taught her about love, faithfulness, forgiveness, provision, protection, peace, and compassion. Every
time David wounded her, she turned to God for healing and
comfort. And the Lord was always there. For His love *was*
perfect.

"The Lord is our shepherd," she whispered to Solomon.
"We have everything we need. He lets us rest in green
meadows; He leads us beside peaceful streams. He renews
our strength. Oh, may He guide us along right paths, bringing honor to His name. Even when we walk through the
dark valley of death, we will not be afraid, for God will be
close beside us. His rod and staff will protect us and we will
be comforted by His presence. The Lord will prepare a feast
for us in the presence of our enemies. He will welcome us as

His guests, anointing our heads with oil. Our cup overflows with blessings." She kissed Solomon. "Surely God's goodness and unfailing love will pursue us all the days of our lives if we give ourselves wholeheartedly to Him. And we will live in the house of the Lord forever."

David summoned her more often than any of his other wives or concubines. Each time he professed his love for her, she knew he spoke from his heart. She knew also that his deepest desire was to please God and walk in all His ways, and she knew how often he failed and grew depressed. Was it any different for her? The more she tried to live a perfect life for God, the more she recognized her failings. Why else were the sacrificial fires burning from morning till night?

She rested in her husband's arms during one of the evenings she was privileged to spend with him and listened to him. "I wonder what God would've done to help us if I'd poured my heart out to Him that day on the wall? What would He have done if I had prayed to Him when I saw you bathing, rather than taking matters into my own hands?" He combed his fingers through her hair.

She closed her eyes. Considering how greatly God had blessed her despite her grievous sin, she couldn't imagine what His plan might have been had she been faithful and obedient. What if David had never seen her bathing? What if he'd never called for her and she'd remained faithful to Uriah? Yet having experienced God's discipline, she knew she had gained a life-changing understanding of redemption and restoration. She now knew beyond a shadow of a doubt how great were God's mercy and lovingkindness, and for that she was oh so thankful. The sweet incense of faith was released when her life and will were crushed.

Lord, I thought I could live my life and be happy without You. I was wrong, so terribly wrong. Forgive me.

And God did.

Everyone knew David loved her, for he treated her with the honor of a first wife. He didn't seem to notice or care about the problems his partiality caused inside the palace. Men and women alike feared Bathsheba's influence and vied for David's attention. David was proud of all his sons, especially Absalom, but the king seemed to have a special affinity for Solomon, who shared his intense love for God. And Bathsheba knew that affinity was a danger. She remained watchful.

God's blessings continued to rain down on Bathsheba, and she bore David a third son, Shimea; a fourth, Shobab; and a fifth, Nathan. David's other wives treated her with grudging honor, for no one wanted to share the same fate as Michal, David's first wife, who was cloistered and given charge over her brother's children, doomed never to have children of her own.

Yet, some of the women found their own revenge. Ahinoam and Maacah planted seeds of suspicion and dissension in their sons. They nurtured the young men's pride and arrogance. They fanned the fires of their ambition, and they failed to instruct their sons in the Law.

Of all those around her, there were only a select few Bathsheba trusted: David, Abigail, her handmaiden, and the prophet Nathan, after whom she had named her fifth son. The prophet had become her friend as well as her counselor.

Caught up in the duties of raising four sons, she had no time for hollow flattery and less time to worry over the manipulations of the other women in the palace. Or of the antics of David's other offspring. Her duty was clear: to raise up her sons to be men of God. She had no power over David and what he did, and she grieved when she saw him shirk his kingly responsibilities. Each year, he seemed to delegate more of his duties to others: her grandfather, Ahithophel; his commander, Joab; his eldest sons, Amnon and Absalom. He spent more and more time writing beautiful songs of praise and worship, pouring his heart out before the Lord, and making plans to build a magnificent temple for the Lord. She knew all these things were good, but what of Israel? What of the people who needed him? What of those who looked to him to lead?

David failed to see the gathering storm.

The prophet Nathan had told her of the cursing to come. She took the word of the Lord to heart and was watchful of what was happening around her. One sin set others in motion. The first stone had tumbled years ago, and an avalanche was coming. She kept her sons close—teaching them about God as she walked with them, teaching them as she sat with them. She tucked them into bed with stories of Creation, the Flood, the patriarchs, the Egyptian enslavement and God's deliverance from it. "Remember the Lord" was her litany.

She knew her sons would face the brunt of the prejudice against her. When they asked painful questions, she answered with the devastating truth. "Yes, your father and I committed adultery. Yes, men died because of me." She had compromised once; she couldn't afford to compromise again. She took every opportunity to speak to her sons of repentance and responsibility, of consequences set in motion when one gives in to sin, of the power of the Lord to uphold the righteous. And she told them of the Lord's great mercy and lovingkindness toward her.

"Whenever you sin—for sin you will—you must repent. You must turn your back on evil and seek God's face. If you do that, God will forgive you."

"And God will make it right," Solomon said.

She smiled sadly. "He will forgive you, but he won't remove the consequences."

"Why not?"

"We must learn to obey."

When Nathan sent word that he wanted to instruct her sons in the Law of the Lord, she seized the opportunity with thanksgiving and sent them off with instructions: "Listen with your hearts, my sons." Once again, God had reached down. And this time He was lifting her sons from a palace of intrigue and setting them down beside His chosen prophet.

+   +   +

Shouting and screaming reverberated throughout the palace as news spread that Amnon, David's eldest son and heir to the throne, had raped his half sister, Tamar. David tore his robe, for he realized he'd believed the tale his son had concocted to gain permission for the girl to attend him in his private chamber. David had sent Tamar to Amnon, never suspecting the young man had improper intentions toward her.

Now Maacah, Tamar's mother, was screaming at him for justice, demanding that Amnon be punished for his crime. How could David agree, when the punishment for rape was death? Could he execute his own son, his heir? When Tamar had cried out in the streets, her brother Absalom had silenced her.

David reminded Maacah of that now. "Woman, if Absalom isn't demanding his brother's blood, why should you? He's taken our daughter into his house and told her to say no more of the matter."

"He's waiting for you to do something!"

"And would you be so quick to demand justice if it were your son who sinned?"

"My son would never take a woman in sin!" Maacah wept hysterically. "This is your fault! It started with your taking that woman!" She could not be silenced. "Your brother's son Jonadab suggested the plan to Amnon, and *you sent my daughter* to Amnon! You sent her, and now she's ruined! What will become of Tamar now? Amnon's sin is on *your* head!"

David wept because he knew she was right.

Those who wanted David to prosper advised him to follow the Law, but David didn't listen.

"How can you ask me to stone my own son? Did I not sin when I took Bathsheba into the palace? Did I not sin when I murdered Uriah? God showed mercy upon me!"

"You repented, my lord the king. Amnon—"

"How can I show less mercy to Amnon, my own flesh and blood?"

"My lord the king . . ."

"I will not pass judgment upon another, when I myself have sinned so grievously. I forgive him and demand that you do likewise!"

Bathsheba covered her face and wept in the privacy of her chamber.

What could a son learn from a father who stole another man's wife and murdered her husband—what else but to believe he could do as he pleased? He had learned to take what he wanted when he wanted it, without counting the cost to anyone.

Oh, God, thus does my sin come to rest again upon me! If not for Your love and mercy, how could I bear to stand and witness what my sins have caused?

Bathsheba mourned for Tamar. She mourned for Maacah, who was inconsolable and embittered. She mourned for Amnon because she knew God would judge him for what he had done. And in the midst of her grief, she felt the accusing glances, heard the whispers. She knew what people were thinking. *What you did all those years ago is the cause of our misery now!*

Absalom's silence made her tremble, for he was no less arrogant than Amnon. In fact, he was even more proud. He'd been praised for his looks and petted since he was a little boy. The older he grew, the more he strutted like a peacock. Would a man like that forgive the rape of his beautiful sister?

Solomon noticed her distress. "What do you fear, Mother?"

"I fear what happens when sin is overlooked." *When the*

sentence for an evil deed isn't executed quickly, the hearts of men are given fully to evil.

Months passed, and nothing happened. David considered the matter resolved and never spoke of it. Bathsheba continued to watch. She hoped David was right, but she continued to do all she could to guard her sons from corruption.

A year passed, and another, as the weeds grew taller among the wheat.

✦   ✦   ✦

"Absalom invited me to his sheepshearing," David told Bathsheba one evening as they took supper alone together. "He's invited all his brothers."

Though alarmed, she kept silent about her misgivings. Absalom had not invited *her* four sons, but she was relieved he hadn't. Absalom hated her because David preferred her over his mother. And he saw her sons as a threat, even though he was next in line as heir to the throne after Amnon.

She poured more wine. "Are you going?"

He shook his head, caressing her fingers as he took the cup. "I'd rather stay here. Besides, why should I burden Absalom with the cost of my retinue? It's better for him if I remain in the palace. The young men will have their fun without me. Amnon will be going as my representative."

She shuddered. "I'm glad my sons won't be going."

"Why aren't they?"

"They weren't invited."

David frowned and thought for a moment. Then he shrugged. "Perhaps Absalom didn't think they'd be interested in such festivities, since they spend so much time with Nathan."

A few days later, Bathsheba was startled by the sound of screaming and wailing. She ran from her room, terrified that something had happened to David. Solomon intercepted her, his face pale, his eyes wide with shock and fear. "A messenger just came and said that Absalom has struck down all the brothers who attended the sheepshearing. Not one of them remains!"

She went cold, her mind racing. If Absalom had dared such a thing, she knew what he would dare next. "Find your brothers and go to your father. Stay at his side!"

Absalom was after the throne, and the only way he could take it would be to wage war against David.

The palace was in an uproar, women screaming and wailing, men standing about in torn garments while David lay prostrate and weeping upon the floor.

More news arrived. Only Amnon was dead. One by one, David's sons rode home on their donkeys, repeating the story of how David's heir had been merry with wine when Absalom set his men upon him, watching in glee as his brother was stabbed repeatedly until dead.

David gathered men to go after Absalom, but his son fled to Geshur and took refuge in the home of his mother's father, King Talmai.

Bathsheba often thought about what had happened at the sheepshearing. She tried to think as her grandfather would. There were three reasons why Absalom would murder Amnon: to avenge his sister, to openly defy his father, and to declare himself heir to the throne of Israel. David's remaining sons were now stricken with fear of Absalom. They knew he was ruthless in his quest for vengeance and power.

Would Absalom have killed David if he had gone to the sheepshearing? Surely a son would stop short of murdering his own father!

David talked continually about going out against him. He talked and talked . . . but did nothing.

✦   ✦   ✦

Three years passed. Reconciled to Amnon's death, David dismissed the notion of war, for his spies reported that Absalom had not gathered an army around him in Geshur. David concluded that Amnon's murder had been an act of revenge over Tamar, not a bid for the throne. Bathsheba knew David's mind was still fixed upon Absalom. Her husband was torn by love for this wayward son and anger over the young man's actions.

"Your son waits to be forgiven," Joab told the king. Bathsheba sensed that her husband was waiting for any excuse to welcome Absalom home again. Without an army and allies, he wouldn't succeed in taking the crown from David, but Bathsheba still didn't feel he was trustworthy. She said nothing against Absalom, of course, knowing anything she said would be misconstrued. What good would come of her speaking her mind when David still grieved over his absence and listened so eagerly for any news of him? No, all she could do was to make certain he knew he did have sons who sought God's favor and would stand with their father against all enemies.

Whenever David sent word he wanted to spend an

evening with her, she made certain Solomon and his brothers joined them for a time. David always enjoyed talking with them, and she wanted him to see and take comfort in his only godly sons.

+ + +

The palace was changing.

David ordered several houses built in an attempt to keep peace among his women. Ahinoam continued to mourn Amnon while Maacah pleaded Absalom's cause so long and loud that David finally refused to see her anymore.

Solomon and his brothers often spent their afternoons with Bathsheba. She loved to hear them talk over the things they were learning from Nathan. They were astute in other areas as well. They knew what was happening in Jerusalem while she, dwelling within the walls of the palace, knew so little. It was her sons who informed her that Absalom would soon be returning to Jerusalem.

"Has your father pardoned him?"

"Not exactly," Solomon said. "I was in court the other day when a Tekoite widow came forward, claiming a clan wanted her to hand over her son who had killed his brother. She said if she did so, they would kill him as well and she would have no sons. Abba agreed to protect the heir. Then he realized the story was a ruse."

"A ruse?"

"Joab put the words in her mouth."

Disturbed, Bathsheba stood and moved away. Joab again. Was Joab sending the king another message: *Bring Absalom back or I stand with him against you?*

FRANCINE RIVERS

"My father would be wise to keep Absalom close so he can watch him," Solomon said.

"Yes, he would." She looked back at him. "Speak with Nathan about this. See what he has to say!" She intended to pray that David would not give in to his volatile emotions again. Joab had manipulated him, but retaliation would serve no purpose.

When David was told that Absalom was coming up the mountain to Jerusalem, he struck a blow against Joab. "Absalom may go to his own house, but he must never come into my presence." David had slammed the door of reconciliation in his son's face in order to put Joab in his place.

When Bathsheba heard what David had done in anger, she grieved. How long before Absalom's pride demanded retribution? And how many would die when he lashed out again? The word of the Lord given through Nathan so many years before stood: the sword would be a constant threat to David's family.

+ + +

It took two years for the fire in Absalom's heart to come out into the open.

"Absalom set fire to Joab's field," Shobab told Bathsheba one afternoon as she talked with her growing sons.

Solomon shook his head. "It's only a matter of time now before Joab comes to Abba and pleads our brother's case," Solomon said grimly.

"If your father reconciles with Absalom, it can only be good for the nation." She wished for an end to familial hostilities. The breech with his eldest surviving son

depressed David and divided the people. Many felt
Absalom justified in killing Amnon because the king had
not acted according to the Law in avenging the rape of
Absalom's sister. Others said David's inaction was a sign of
indecision, not mercy. An indecisive king was a weak king,
open to the schemes and machinations of enemies, and
David had enemies on all sides. Only God could protect him
and keep him on the throne.

"No good will come of this, Mother," Solomon said. "If
Absalom dared to set fire to Joab's field, what more will he
dare besides?"

"Are you implying he will stand against the king?"

"He's too shrewd to be so open. And he needs allies. Joab
won't stand with him now. But you know better than I how
proud Absalom is."

Shimea laughed. "I heard he weighs his hair every time
he cuts it!"

"His beauty has made him vain," Bathsheba said quietly.

"Everyone is charmed by his good looks, but he's filled
with deceit. Abba ordered him to his own house two years
ago, and that command hasn't changed. Two years is more
than enough time to stoke the fires in Absalom's belly."

Bathsheba searched for reasons to hope for peace. "Absalom is heir to the throne. He needs to be patient. He has
nothing to gain by dividing a nation he will one day rule."

Solomon laughed without humor. "The only time I've
seen my brother show patience was during the two years he
plotted the murder of Amnon."

She rose. "We will speak no more of this now." She
couldn't bear it. "Keep your eyes open and tell me what you

see and hear." She knew if Absalom ever challenged David and won, her life and the lives of her sons would be forfeit.

Solomon bowed his head. Bending down, he kissed her cheek. He started to say something more, but she put her fingers over his lips. "Speak with the prophet Nathan about your concerns," she said. "Seek the counsel of the Lord."

"Yes, Mother."

She kissed him and each of her sons and watched them leave.

Lord God, protect my sons. Let the sins of the past fall on my head and not on theirs.

✦   ✦   ✦

David heard Joab's plea and allowed Absalom to come before him, but the kiss he bestowed upon his son was less in affection than official pardon. Soon after, Bathsheba heard that Absalom had taken to riding in a horse-drawn chariot with fifty men running before him as though he were already king. He rose early and went down to stand by the gate road, intercepting those who came to Jerusalem to have their cases heard before the king, telling them he was the only one who would listen and judge justly, and making promises only a king could fulfill.

When he came before David and asked to go to Hebron to fulfill a vow he'd made, David let him go, too preoccupied with his own comforts and pleasure to sense Absalom's true motive.

Absalom left Jerusalem with two hundred invited guests and declared himself king in Hebron. "All Israel has joined Absalom in a conspiracy against you," David was told by messengers.

And now Absalom was on his way to Jerusalem, with an army, to take the throne from his father.

+   +   +

Women and servants scrambled around the palace, gathering what they would need for a journey. David had given orders that his household was to leave Jerusalem before Absalom could arrive with his army. Only ten concubines would stay behind and keep the palace in order.

Bathsheba kept her sons close by her side as David led them out with all his people after him. As they stopped on the outskirts of the city, six hundred men joined forces with them, foreigners who had come to see the king. David told them they should leave, that this wasn't their battle. Bathsheba was relieved when they swore allegiance to him and remained. David would need all the men he could muster if they were to survive.

Men and women were weeping and wailing as they crossed the stream of Kidron, heading out toward the wilderness. Zadok, the high priest, and all the Levites followed David with the Ark of God, but when David heard about it, he told them to go back to Jerusalem.

"If the Lord sees fit, He will bring me back to see the Ark and the Tabernacle again. But if He is through with me, then let Him do what seems best to Him." He walked barefoot and wept, keeping his head covered as he grieved over his rebellious son.

As David led his people up the Mount of Olives, a messenger came, dusty and exhausted. "Ahithophel is among the conspirators!"

Bathsheba dropped to her knees and cried out. She

covered her head with dust. She wept, remembering her grandfather, the man she'd loved as a child and a young woman—his laughter, his love, his tender devotion to his family. Ahithophel was at last taking his vengeance against her and David. She felt David's eyes upon her and put her head against her thighs, ashamed of what her love for him had caused.

She put her hands over her head when she heard David cry out in anguish and wrath. "O Lord, let Ahithophel give Absalom foolish advice!"

Counselors and advisers surrounded David, all speaking at once, drawing him away from her. Bathsheba felt strong arms lift her and heard Solomon's fierce whisper. "God will protect us."

"My fault," she choked. "This is all my fault."

He embraced her, protecting her from those who stared. "Should the sins of everyone be laid at your feet?"

She shook with grief. "The avalanche started years ago, my son, and the whole mountain is coming down on us this time!"

"Each man makes his own decision, Mother. Ahithophel's sin will rest upon his own head."

She shook her head. "He's your great-grandfather."

"He requested leave and went home to Giloh years ago, using the excuse that Israel was at peace. Now we know the real reason for his departure. Treachery!" Solomon drew back while still giving her support. "If there's anything I've learned from all this, Mother, it's not to trust anyone, even someone of your own blood."

"You can trust me. You can trust your father."

"I love you, Mother, and I trust you, but what power have you? And I love my father, but the king lost touch with his people years ago."

Bathsheba didn't reprimand her son for his words because he said them with sorrow and not condemnation. She thought of her grandfather again, and her heart quaked. All these years he had pretended to be at peace with David while seeking an opportunity to destroy him.

Oh, if only I'd been stronger and wiser . . .

She stopped the thought. *If only . . . if only . . .* What was the use in such thinking? It was too late to wish she'd done things differently. They were all stained with sin, and sacrifices merely covered it with another's blood.

Oh, God of mercy, how I long to be free of my sins, to be an innocent child again, as white as snow.

Had Ahithophel thought through his vengeance? Could he hate her and David so much that he would destroy himself to get even? If he succeeded in setting Absalom on the throne, David would die. She would die. And the lives of Ahithophel's four great-grandsons would be forfeit as well! Angry and desperate, she prayed with every step that her husband's prayer would be answered and God would confuse her grandfather's advice to Absalom. For without God's favor, all would be lost. Ahithophel knew more about waging a successful war than any man in the kingdom, including Joab, who now marched with David, protecting him against the son with whom he had once schemed. Joab with his murderous pride. Joab with his hidden motives and deadly ambition! He'd pulled David in a dozen directions over the past three decades!

She looked up at Solomon. "You and your brothers must go and stand with your father."

"We are standing with him."

"No. Stay *close* to him. Protect him from Absalom and anyone else who might harm him. If the king falls, we all fall." Tears blinded her. "Show David he has sons he can trust!"

As she walked alone among the throng leaving Jerusalem with David, she remembered conversations from years past around her father's campfire at En-gedi. *"Kill Saul,"* Abishai had once said. *"Strike the shepherd and the sheep will scatter,"* Joab had advised. David had left the fire, refusing to listen, and her grandfather had discussed the matter with her father after the others followed. *"Joab's advice is shrewd. Saul's death would put an end to this war and place David on the throne. But there would be no blessing for David if he kills the Lord's anointed."*

No blessing.

The last thing her grandfather would want now was blessing on the house of David. And what better way to avenge his so-called honor than by setting son against father? Ahithophel would destroy a nation because of his pride. Were all men so evil-bent, so lacking in the ability to forgive? What right had man to judge what God redeemed? Her mother had warned her years ago that her grandfather would never let the matter go. She had hoped and prayed that he would take a different course. She wept now as she saw that Ahithophel had only pretended to forgive. She knew he would advise Absalom to pursue and kill David. And if successful, Absalom's kingdom would be cursed as well, for what nation could prosper through a son's shedding his own father's blood? The house of David would fall.

Oh, Lord, Lord, that one night of sin could bring such sorrow!

No matter what happened, someone she loved was going to die.

Let it be Ahithophel, Lord. She wept at uttering such a prayer. *Let it be my grandfather and not my husband and sons.*

+ + +

As David led his people to Bahurim, a man named Shimei from the family of Saul came out and shouted curses at him. The man kept pace, picked up stones, and hurled them, along with his bitter words, at David and his servants. "Get out of here, you murderer!" he screamed in rage. "You scoundrel! The Lord is paying you back for murdering Saul and his family. You stole his throne, and now the Lord has given it to your son Absalom. At last you will taste some of your own medicine, you murderer!"

Abishai drew his sword. "Why should this dead dog curse my lord the king? Let me go over and cut off his head!"

David cried out in anger and despair. "No! What am I going to do with you sons of Zeruiah! If the Lord has told him to curse me, who am I to stop him?" He wept and shouted, "My own son is trying to kill me. Shouldn't this relative of Saul have even more reason to do so? Leave him alone and let him curse, for the Lord has told him to do it. And perhaps the Lord will see that I am being wronged and will bless me because of these curses."

David continued along the road, wincing at every word Shimei laid upon his head. He felt stones strike him. He tasted the dust the Benjaminite kicked up.

When the people grew too weary to go farther, he gave orders to camp. He'd done all he could. He had sent another of his military advisers, Hushai, to pretend allegiance to Absalom. He instructed Hushai to counter whatever counsel Ahithophel gave. David had also sent Zadok the priest and his sons back into Jerusalem to act as messengers for Hushai. If there was any hope for escape, Hushai would see that David got word. Everything rested in God's hands. The outcome would be according to God's will.

I will die if my son pursues me now, Lord. I'm too tired to go on, and my people need rest. Help me. Oh, God, help me!

He took off his crown and held it in his hands. "Oh, Lord, hear me as I pray," he whispered. "Don't hide Yourself from my plea. Please answer my prayers. Trouble is all around me because of a grudge held against me for sins I committed long ago. My heart is anguished." Closing his eyes, he gripped the crown tightly. "God, I'm terrified of death. Mine and all those I love. I'm shaking like a boy untried by battle. I wish I had wings like a dove so I could escape." He swallowed. "Confuse Ahithophel's tongue. All these years I thought he was my friend, and he's been plotting against me." He wept as he raked one hand back through his hair, dangling the crown in his other hand. "Ahithophel. My friend. My companion all these years. We had sweet fellowship together during those years in the wilderness."

He ground his teeth, running his hand around the back of

his neck. "All these years his words have been as smooth as butter, and war has been in his heart. He talked of peace with a drawn sword behind his back. He has fanned my son's ambitions and set him against me." He shook as rage heated his blood. "Send them into the pit of destruction, Lord! Let him go down alive into Sheol!"

David let out his breath slowly, striving for control of his emotions. He must be calm to give the people courage. He must think. He must act wisely. *What a fool I've been, allowing myself to become soft and letting others run the kingdom!* He turned the crown slowly in his hands and placed it back on his head, then rubbed his face, feeling the dust and grit of travel rubbing his skin. *Oh, God, I never asked to be king.* He would have been happier as a shepherd, singing psalms and looking at the stars in the heavens. He would have been happier as a poor man with only one wife.

Men plan, but God prevails.

With a sigh, David stood. "I will trust in You, oh, Lord. I will trust in You. Do with me as you will."

✦　✦　✦

Hushai reported to Zadok, and the priest sent his two sons to David. "Quick! Cross the Jordan tonight! Ahithophel is advising Absalom to pursue immediately, overtake you, and kill you. Hushai advises you not to spend the night in the plains of the wilderness, but to speedily cross over lest you and all the people with you be swallowed up!"

And there was more news, bitter and reminiscent of Nathan's prophecy so many years before. "Acting on Ahithophel's advice, Absalom has taken your ten concubines up onto the roof. He is sleeping with them before all Israel."

David felt the hair on the back of his neck rise. He could imagine Ahithophel's face ravaged by hatred, could imagine his thoughts: *Remember all those years ago when you stood upon your roof and looked down upon my granddaughter? Remember how you took her and defiled her? How you brought shame upon my household? Now I will watch your son defile your women and bring shame upon your household before all Israel!*

David roused the people and they traveled on to Mahanaim, where they were met by men from Rabbah and Ammon and offered beds, basins, and earthen vessels filled with wheat, barley, flour, parched grain and seeds, beans, lentils, honey and curds, sheep, and cheese from the herd. David's people ate their fill and rested.

David counted his men. He set up captains over thousands and captains over hundreds. Dividing his army into three parts, he sent one-third of his fighting force with Joab, one-third with Abishai, and one-third with Ittai the Gittite. Then, with a heavy heart, he prepared to go out to war against his own son.

The people protested loudly against his going out with them. "You must not go. If we have to turn and run—and even if half of us die—it will make no difference to Absalom's troops; they will be looking only for you. You are worth ten thousand of us, and it is better that you stay here in the city and send us help if we need it."

David listened and once more stepped down. "If you think that's the best plan, I'll do it." He gave orders to

Joab, Abishai, and Ittai in front of the army. "For my sake, deal gently with young Absalom." Then he remained standing at the gate as the men passed by him and went out to battle.

Once again, David remained behind while others fought for him. But this time he did it because it was what the people wanted and not what he wanted for himself.

✦   ✦   ✦

The watchman from the tower called down. "A runner is coming!"

David paced. "If he is alone, he has news," he muttered to himself. When the watchman shouted down again that another man was spotted coming swiftly after, David's heart quickened in dread.

"The first man runs like Ahimaaz son of Zadok!" the watchman called again.

David clenched and unclenched his hands. "He is a good man and comes with good news."

Ahimaaz called out before he reached the open gate, "All is well!" David's heart leaped as the young man fell to his knees before him and bowed his face to the ground. "Blessed be the Lord your God," he gasped, "who has handed over the rebels who dared to stand against you."

"What about young Absalom? Is he all right?"

Ahimaaz raised his head in surprise. His eyes flickered and he bowed his head again. "When Joab told me to come, there was a lot of commotion. But I didn't know what was happening."

Why did Ahimaaz hide his face? David's heart beat harder. He raised his head as the watchman cried out again.

Another messenger raced toward them. "Wait here," David ordered Ahimaaz.

The second messenger arrived, breathless and dusty. "I have good news for my lord the king. Today the Lord has rescued you from all those who rebelled against you."

"What about young Absalom? Is he all right?" David demanded.

The Cushite's eyes flashed. "May all of your enemies, both now and in the future, be as that young man is!"

David's heart turned over, for he knew. "My son! My son is dead!" he cried out in anguish. "O my son Absalom! My son, my son Absalom! If only I could have died instead of you! O Absalom, my son, my son!"

Stumbling up the stairs into the chamber above the gate, David collapsed in grief.

✦   ✦   ✦

David didn't rouse himself when the door of his chamber opened. He didn't raise his head until Joab's voice flooded over him in a rage.

"We saved your life today and the lives of your sons, your daughters, and your wives and concubines!" Joab's face was red, his hand clenched on the handle of his sword. "Yet you act like this, making us feel ashamed, as though we had done something wrong. You seem to love those who hate you and hate those who love you. You have made it clear today that we mean nothing to you. If Absalom had lived and all of us had died, you would be pleased!"

David hated him and saw in the man's eyes that he had been behind Absalom's death. And was glad of it. "He was my son, my heir!" Had he not ordered Joab before witnesses to treat his son gently? But Joab always did what he thought best, with no regard for others—or for what was right. He was a man who served his own ambitions.

And David saw death in the man's hot eyes.

"*Get up!*" Joab shouted at him. "Now *go out there* and congratulate the troops, for I swear by the Lord that if you don't, not a single one of them will remain here tonight. Then you will be worse off than you have ever been!"

Anger filled David. His body shook as he strove to calm himself, to control the impulse to attack the man. If he didn't do what Joab said, what would it cost the kingdom? He looked into his commander's eyes and knew that if he didn't get up, Joab would be the one to strike, for he made no attempt to hide his anger or disgust.

David rose and crossed the room. He stood in front of Joab and stared into his eyes. "Did you kill him because he burned your field?" A muscle jerked in Joab's cheek as he glared back, silent. David's lip curled. Even if he hadn't, Joab had still ignored the command of the king.

And David knew there was nothing he could do about it. Not now. Once again, it had been Joab who led the army to victory, while the king had waited within the city walls.

Joab stepped back and inclined his head. He had the eyes of a coiled snake.

David didn't give him the chance to strike. Stifling his anger and grief, he went out and sat by the gate. One by one, his warriors came out to see him, and he thanked each of them properly for saving his kingdom.

And then David took his household back to Jerusalem.

+ + +

Bathsheba sat in her chamber and waited. Would David blame her for the death of his son Absalom? Her grandfather had been behind the conspiracy to kill David and take the throne. Did he blame her now?

Days passed and she didn't see him. Nor did the king summon any other woman.

Then, one day, the door opened, and without being announced he entered her room. She rose, her heart in her throat. He looked thinner, his face lined with suffering, streaks of gray at his temples. She took several steps toward him and then went down on her knees, bowing her head until her forehead touched the floor. "Oh, David, I'm so sorry." She began to weep.

His hand rested gently on her head. "I don't blame you for Ahithophel's actions."

She raised her head and looked into his eyes. Amazed, she saw that he still loved her. "Oh, David." He went down beside her and she went into his arms. He held her so tightly, she hurt. She put her head against his chest and felt him kiss the back of her neck.

"I have news," he whispered against her hair, his arms tightening even more. "When Absalom took Hushai's advice to wait, Ahithophel went home and hanged himself."

She trembled violently. God had heard and answered her prayers. *"Ahithophel's sin will rest upon his own head,"* Solomon had said to her as they fled from Absalom. Her grandfather had judged and, by his own measure, had been judged.

David nuzzled her neck, kissing the sensitive curve and

making her tremble. His breath was warm against her flesh. She heard the hard swift pounding of his heart.

"I've decided Solomon will be heir to the throne." She drew back sharply and looked up at him, afraid. He cupped her face. "I've decided. Do you want to know why? The others have nursed their sons on ambition and made them hungry for power." She saw the grief in his eyes. "I swear to you, Bathsheba, it will be *your* son who wears the crown."

"But who am I that you would—"

"Of all my wives and concubines, only you have whole-heartedly sought the Lord."

Her eyes filled. "Where else could I go after what I'd done and all the pain that's come from it?"

David kissed the tears that streaked her face. "Maybe it's only those who've made such chaos of their lives who can understand the heights and depths of God's mercy." He kissed her lips. "I was fond of you because you were the daughter of my friend. I lusted after you and took you because of your beauty. I have loved you for the pleasure you've given me and the peace I feel in your company." He drew back and took her hands.

They stood together. His gaze never left hers as he lifted her hands and kissed each palm. "But I love you most of all for the loving wife you've been to me and the mother you are to my sons. You have raised up four men who love the Lord and seek His face, sons I'm proud of, sons I . . ." His voice broke.

She put her arms around him and comforted him, knowing what he wanted to say but couldn't.

She had raised up sons he could trust.

JUST before David's return to Jerusalem, another
rebellion had threatened to tear the nation into factions as
Sheba, a Benjaminite, called the men of Israel to war against
David. His call to arms ignited the discord that had been
festering between the ten tribes of Israel and David's own
tribe, Judah. Only the men of Judah clung to their king.

Now David instructed Amasa to mobilize his army, but
Joab murdered him and took command of David's army
once again, leading the warriors out against Sheba.
Trapping the rebel at Abel-beth-maacah, he laid siege to the
city until a woman gathered the elders and convinced them
to toss Sheba over the wall, saving the city from Joab.

Years later, the Philistines came out against Israel, and
David led the nation into battle again. He was old and
weary, and the men protested. "You are not going out into

battle again! Why should we risk snuffing out the light of Israel!"

David relented, and his men went into battle without him. During the war that ensued, his mighty men struck down Goliath's brothers, thus wiping out the last descendants of the titan.

Even while David wrote psalms of praise for the Lord, his strong tower and mighty fortress, he sinned against the Lord by taking a census of his fighting men. His pride and ambition led him to count the people so that he could glory in the size of his army, its power and defenses—rather than trusting in God's ability to give them victory regardless of their number. Was it by man's strength his kingdom stood?

When David recognized his sin, he begged for God's forgiveness. The Lord gave him a choice: three years of famine, three months of fleeing from his enemies, or three days of plague. "Let us fall into the hands of the Lord," David said, "for His mercy is great." He chose the plague.

Seventy thousand people died because David had counted his men and gloried in their numbers. Then the Lord relented and said, "Stop! That is enough!" David saw God's death angel sheathe his sword on the threshing floor of Araunah the Jebusite, and he shook in awe. David bought Araunah's threshing floor and oxen and built an altar there, presenting burnt offerings and communion sacrifices to the Lord, who had stopped the destruction of Israel.

One day the Temple would stand on the same spot.

✦ ✦ ✦

Bathsheba watched her beloved husband growing older. His hair was gray, the lines deepening in his still handsome face. His shoulders drooped as though the weight of Israel were on his shoulders. He walked more slowly through the corridors of his palace, and he seldom visited his concubines. His wives continued to come to him with their complaints, pressing their sons forward for his notice until David allowed some to assume duties.

On occasion, David would come to Bathsheba's quarters and spend an afternoon with her. "I was once as swift as an eagle, but now my legs weigh like tree trunks, keeping me planted firmly on the ground."

She smiled up at him as she rubbed his feet. "We're all getting older, my love." When he shivered, she put a blanket around his shoulders.

He took her hand and kissed it. "You're as beautiful to me now as you were as a young woman."

"And you're as charming as ever." She rose and kissed him with the affection of a couple that had weathered many storms over the decades. "You're still shivering."

"The hot blood of my youth has grown cold."

"I don't love you any less."

"My servants have found a way to keep me warm."

She smiled wryly. "So I heard." They'd scoured the land to find the most beautiful young virgin to sleep with him. "Did you plant the idea in their heads, you old rogue?"

"Abishag is beautiful to behold, but that's all I do—look. I'm past all the rest."

"If I could've held you to me alone, I would have."

"And if I'd been wiser at a younger age . . ." He sighed. "If, if . . ." He shook his head. "I knew the Law as well as any man could. I daresay that even if we had the Law written upon our hearts, we would still be incapable of staying out of trouble."

"You have always been a man after God's own heart."

"I'm beset by failure on every side. An adulterer, a murderer, a—"

She put her fingers over his lips. "God loves you because you repented every time you realized you'd sinned. You *grieved*. You *tried* to do right. God knows you are only a man, my love."

"A man who has hurt everyone he loves and cost the lives of countless thousands." He shook his head, his eyes filling with tears. "Why did God do it? Of all the men in Israel, why did God choose *me* to be king?"

She knelt in front of him and rested her head in his lap. She smiled and closed her eyes as he combed his fingers through her hair. "Because you're the only man who would ask that question."

+ + +

Bathsheba knew that Haggith was encouraging her son, Adonijah, to claim his rights as the next heir, for he had been born next after Absalom. When Adonijah procured chariots and horses and recruited fifty men to run in front of him, behaving before all Israel as though he were already king, just as Absalom had done all those years before, she became afraid. Was another rebellion brewing?

David said nothing about Adonijah's activities, and Bathsheba held her tongue. But she wondered. Had David forgotten his promise to make Solomon king? If Adonijah became king, she and her sons would die the day David did, for Adonijah was as arrogant as Absalom had been in his public posturing. When she heard from her sons that Adonijah had parlayed with Joab and Abiathar the priest and that they were lending him their support, she knew it wouldn't be long before he proclaimed himself king and had the backing to uphold his claim.

She took her fear of the future before the Lord. She fasted and prayed, and waited for Him to answer.

Adonijah went to the sacrificial feast of sheep, oxen, and fattened calves near En-rogel. He invited all of David's sons to go with him—all but Solomon and his brothers, the prophet Nathan, the priest Benaiah, and the warriors who remained loyal to the king.

Bathsheba knew war was again at hand. Perhaps this was God's final judgment upon her and David for their sins.

Nathan came to her, grim of countenance, his eyes fierce and alive in his ancient face. "Did you realize that Haggith's son, Adonijah, has made himself king and that our lord David doesn't even know about it?"

"I've been praying."

"If you want to save your own life and the life of your son Solomon, follow my counsel. Go at once to King David and say to him, 'My lord, didn't you promise me that my son Solomon would be the next king and would sit upon your throne? Then why has Adonijah become king?' And while you are still talking with him, I will come and confirm everything you have said."

"I will do it," she said, trembling at what might happen if David had forgotten his promise. Would he think she was just like all the other women in his life, scrambling for power for her sons? Yet, what choice had she? Power in the wrong hands would bring death to her entire family.

She prayed feverishly as she hurried along the corridor to the king's chambers. "I must speak with the king on a matter of great importance," she told his guard. He bowed his head to her and went to seek the permission of the king, returning soon after and opening the door for her.

As Bathsheba entered, she saw the beautiful Shunammite girl, Abishag, serving the king his morning meal. The girl looked up, her lovely face lighting with a sweet smile, inclining her head in respectful greeting. Bathsheba had liked her from their first meeting. Abishag had been a shepherdess over her father's flock before she'd been brought to Jerusalem to serve the king. The loving young Shunammite had many things in common with the old king, especially her faith.

Bathsheba went down on her knees, bowing her face to the ground before her husband, the king.

David roused himself. "What can I do for you, Bathsheba?"

Her heart thundered as she prayed, *Oh, Lord, don't let David see me as he does the others*. She lifted her head and trembled as she spoke. "My lord, you vowed to me by the Lord your God that my son Solomon would be the next king and would sit on your throne. But instead, Adonijah has become the new king, and you do not even know about it. He has sacrificed many oxen, fattened calves, and sheep, and he has invited all your sons and Abiathar the priest and Joab, the commander of the army."

David sat up, his eyes suddenly fierce.

"But he did not invite your servant Solomon. And now, my lord the king, all Israel is waiting for your decision as to who will become king after you. If you do not act, my son Solomon and I will be treated as criminals as soon as you are dead."

"My lord the king," the guard said from the doorway, "Nathan the prophet is here to see you. He said it is a matter of gravest import."

"Let him enter!" David said, breathing heavily, his face tense and red. He waved Abishag away impatiently. "Go, Bathsheba. Leave me!"

Striving to control her emotions, she hurried out of his chamber. She paced and prayed while she waited outside. *Oh, Lord of mercy, let him heed Your prophet.* She clenched her hands and stood, eyes closed. *Oh, God, move David's heart to remember his promise. I know I'm unworthy. I know I'm unworthy, but please save my sons. Set Your servant Solomon upon the throne.*

"Call Bathsheba!" David roared, and her heart stopped. It began pounding hard and fast as she hastened toward the door.

The guard opened it for her. "I am here, my lord the king."

David was standing. "As surely as the Lord lives, who has rescued me from every danger, today I decree that your son Solomon will be the next king and will sit on my throne, just as I swore to you before the Lord, the God of Israel."

Bathsheba dropped to her knees and bowed her face to the ground, weeping as she spoke from her heart. "May my lord King David live forever!"

David called for Zadok the priest, Benaiah, and Nathan the prophet, and gave them instructions. "Take Solomon and my officers down to Gihon Spring. Solomon is to ride on my personal mule. There Zadok the priest and Nathan the prophet are to anoint him king over Israel. Then blow the trumpets and shout, 'Long live King Solomon!' When you bring him back here, he will sit on my throne. He will succeed me as king, for I have appointed him to be ruler over Israel and Judah."

"Amen!" the priests said, their eyes glowing as they glanced at one another.

The old lion had finally awakened.

✦   ✦   ✦

Bathsheba's heart was in her throat as she stood with members of David's household and watched Zadok take the horn of oil from the sacred tent, anointing her son king. David was smiling, two men giving him support while Abishag stood nearby.

As Nathan turned toward him, David removed his crown and held it out. "Give it to Bathsheba."

The old prophet's eyes lit up. As he handed the crown to Bathsheba, her eyes welled with tears at being honored so before the people. David smiled and inclined his head toward her. She smiled back, turned, and placed the crown on their son's head.

The people shouted joyfully, *"Long live King Solomon!"* Over and over again, they cried out their blessings. Some played flutes. Thousands danced in the streets and sang, making such revelry the earth shook with their jubilee.

Bathsheba laughed and cried, her heart so full she felt it

would burst. She looked from David to her son. The anointing oil dripped down Solomon's face into his beard. *"Beloved of the Lord!"* Who would have ever thought *her* son would be king over Israel! *Oh, Lord God of Israel, merciful redeemer, lifter of my soul, look what You have done for me! Look what You have done!* She put her hands over her heart and bowed low.

When Solomon was seated on the royal throne, David, near exhaustion, bowed down to him. "Blessed be the Lord, the God of Israel, who today has chosen someone to sit on my throne while I am still alive to see it."

A messenger came, informing David that Adonijah's guests had fled when they heard the people celebrating Solomon's coronation. Now, out of fear for their lives, all were clamoring to be first to sing Solomon's praises and bow down before him. David rose. When Bathsheba started to rise, he shook his head. "Enjoy this day, my love. See what God has done." He was assisted from the room by two male attendants, with Abishag following.

Another messenger came, throwing himself on his face before Solomon. "My lord the king!"

"Rise, and speak your message."

"Adonijah is afraid of you and has fled to the sacred tent for protection. He said, 'Let Solomon swear today that he will not kill me!'"

Bathsheba held her breath as she saw Solomon's eyes darken and his hands tighten on the arms of the throne. "If he proves himself to be loyal, he will not be harmed. But if he does not, he will die." She breathed easier as her son sent guards to get his brother and bring him to the throne room.

The elder brother bowed to her son, but he didn't throw himself on the floor as others had done before him. He inclined his head, but did not bend his back. Her son watched Adonijah closely, his eyes narrowed. "Go on home, Adonijah. Go and remember my warning."

There was a hushed silence as Adonijah turned and walked out of the throne room. Bathsheba knew there would be trouble ahead if a way to peace between the brothers could not be found.

✦ ✦ ✦

As Solomon took over the responsibilities of kingship, David's health declined. Bathsheba came each morning to sit with him, but it was Abishag who was in constant attendance, seeing to his most basic needs.

Bathsheba's heart ached as she watched the man she loved slip away. She knew it was close to the end when he summoned Solomon from his duties. The king brought his brothers Shobab, Shimea, and Nathan with him.

Solomon bowed down before his father. David put his hand on his son's head. "My son," he rasped, tears in his eyes. "Sit and we will talk as we used to." He smiled at the four men surrounding him.

Reaching out, David took Bathsheba's hand. "I am going where everyone on earth must someday go."

Solomon and his brothers began to weep.

"Take courage," David said, directing his words to Solomon, "and be a man. Observe the requirements of the Lord your God and follow all His ways. Keep each of the laws, commands, regulations, and stipulations written in the Law of Moses so that you will be successful in all you do and wherever you go. If you do this, then the Lord will keep the promise He made to me: 'If your descendants live as they should and follow Me faithfully with all their heart and soul, one of them will always sit on the throne of Israel.'"

Bathsheba closed her eyes, her throat constricting as she heard the encroaching weakness in David's voice. She was losing him. After all these years, he was leaving her.

David took his hand from hers and stirred on his couch, restless, hurried. "And there is something else. You know that Joab son of Zeruiah murdered my two army commanders, Abner son of Ner and Amasa son of Jether. He pretended that it was an act of war, but it was done in a time of peace, staining his belt and sandals with the blood of war. Do with him what you think best, but don't let him die in peace!"

"Yes, Abba."

"Be kind to the sons of Barzillai. . . ."

"Yes, Abba."

"And remember Shimei son of Gera, the man from Bahurim in Benjamin. He cursed me with a terrible curse as I was fleeing to Mahanaim. When he came down to meet me at the Jordan River, I swore by the Lord that I would not kill him. But that oath does not make him innocent. You are a wise man, and you will know how to arrange a bloody death for him."

Bathsheba shuddered, but she said nothing as David sank back, breathing heavily. Turning his head, he looked at her, pain etching his face. "Ah, my love," he said softly. His breath came out in one long, deep sigh of peace and his body relaxed.

Bathsheba rocked back and forth, her anguish so deep, the tears gathered like a hot stone in her chest. When Abishag leaned forward and gently ran her hand down David's face, closing his eyes, Bathsheba's grief broke free. Keening, she ripped the neckline of her dress and pressed her hands over her chest, feeling as though her heart had been torn from her. "David! *Daaaa . . . vid!*"

Her sons rose and surrounded her like sentinels. And King Solomon's hand was gentle upon her shoulder.

✦   ✦   ✦

David was buried with great ceremony in the city named after him. As the people mourned him, Bathsheba prayed they would remember the good he had done for them and the heart he had for God rather than the mistakes he had made.

Solomon sat easily upon the throne, his mind trained in administration by Nathan and the priests. But his throne was not yet secure. Enemies were gathering.

One afternoon, Adonijah came to see her. "My mother sends you greetings," he said, bowing to her for the first time she could remember.

Haggith had always been as ambitious for her sons as Maacah. "Have you come to make trouble?" Should she remind him to heed the warning Solomon had given for his own sake? or hear him out to know better what was going on in his mind?

"No," he said quickly. "I come in peace. In fact, I have a favor to ask of you."

A favor? She tilted her head. "What is it?" she said cautiously.

"As you know, the kingdom was mine."

She stiffened, her heart thumping. Did he mean to remind her that he had been next in line after Absalom? Or was he referring to his rebellion? He had managed to gain the backing of powerful men in the kingdom, men who had encouraged him to declare himself king. They'd all mistakenly thought David too tired and ill to notice. And even if the king did know, they figured he would not be able to muster enough strength to stop the rebellion.

Adonijah spread his hands as though to show he had no weapons. "Everyone expected me to be the next king. But the tables were turned, and everything went to my brother instead; for that is the way the Lord wanted it."

She watched his face for some sign of subterfuge, but he seemed to accept David's wishes. *The Lord wanted it.* The Lord had chosen Solomon to reign—Solomon, her son. *I am still amazed, Lord, amazed that You would choose the son of an adulterous woman. . . .*

"So now," Adonijah said, drawing her attention back to him, "I have just one favor to ask of you. Please don't turn me down."

"What is it?"

He stepped closer and went down on one knee, his face taut, his eyes dark. "Speak to King Solomon on my behalf, for I know he will do anything you request. Ask him to give me Abishag, the girl from Shunem, as my wife."

Abishag! She searched his face and thought the emotions

she saw there must be love, for she could feel his intensity and could see his hunger.

Oh, Lord, is this the way to bring peace between brothers? If Solomon gives his brother Abishag, will there be peace between them? Will that tender girl soften this man's heart? Oh, let it be so!

"All right," she said slowly and saw his eyes catch fire. "I will speak to the king for you."

Adonijah said not another word, but when he rose, his lips curved in a strange smile of triumph.

✦　✦　✦

Bathsheba dressed in her finest attire before going to her son, the king. She waited while he was told she requested an audience with him. When she was admitted, Solomon rose from his throne and came down the dais to her. She blushed as he bowed down before her, his entire court watching him. Smiling, he took her hand and led her up the steps with him. "Bring another throne for my mother," he commanded.

"You show me too much honor, my son," she whispered as a second throne was set to the right of his.

"The people must understand my respect for you." He smiled as he seated her first. "Does the Law not say, 'Honor your father *and* mother'?"

Tongues would never be silenced where she was concerned, and she would not be able to protect him against the prejudice held against her. Hadn't her sons been scorned and excluded over the years? It would be best if she went into seclusion. Perhaps if she was not seen, she would be forgotten, and the stains of her sin would not seep into Solomon's reign. "I hold no grudges, my son."

"Nor do I, Mother." His eyes glittered. "But boundaries need to be established. My father loved you and treated you as his queen, and so shall you be treated by all." He let out his breath and smiled again. "Now tell me what is on your mind, for I know you wouldn't have come without good reason."

She laid her hand upon his. "I have one small request to make of you." She hoped it would bring peace between him and his brother as well as kinder feelings between her and the other widows of David. "I hope you won't turn me down."

"What is it, my mother? You know I won't refuse you."

She relaxed. "Then let your brother Adonijah marry Abishag, the girl from Shunem."

Silence followed her words, such a look of shock on Solomon's face that her heart stopped. When he jerked his hand from beneath hers, she drew in a startled breath, confused by his growing wrath.

"How can you possibly ask me to give Abishag to Adonijah?" His voice was low and intense. "You might as well be asking me to give him the kingdom! You know that he is my older brother, and that he has Abiathar the priest and Joab son of Zeruiah on his side. If he were to claim one of my father's concubines as his own, it would be tantamount to claiming the kingship!" He bolted from the throne. "May God strike me dead if Adonijah has not sealed his fate with this request!"

Oh no! Oh, God, what have I done now?

"The Lord has confirmed me and placed me on the throne of my father, David." Solomon spoke for all to hear. "He has established my dynasty as he promised. So as surely as the Lord lives, Adonijah will die this very day!"

Bathsheba uttered a soft cry. She held her hand out to stop Solomon before he could say more, but he ignored her and called out for his most trustworthy servant, Benaiah. "Go *now* and execute Adonijah."

"Yes, my lord the king!" Benaiah drew his sword and strode from the room.

Bathsheba lowered her hands to her lap and bent her head as Solomon called for another of his servants and commanded him to bring Abiathar the priest to him at once. When Solomon turned to her, she raised her head, her eyes awash with tears. "I didn't know. I never thought this would happen."

"Return to your chamber, Mother." His voice was gentle again. "Rest. I'll talk with you later."

Thus dismissed, she rose, trembling. Frowning, he put his hand beneath her arm. "Mother," he said softly.

"I will be all right," she said in a quavering voice.

"Take my mother to her chamber," he told his servant and released her into another's care.

Bathsheba felt everyone's eyes upon her. Lifting her head, she walked with grave dignity from the room. She said nothing as she walked along the corridors. Her son's servant released her to the eunuch in charge of the women's quarters. "My lady," he said, frowning. She shook her head and walked away from him, entering her private quarters.

Her handmaiden came to her. "My lady! What is it? What's happened?"

Bathsheba put a hand to her forehead. "Leave me."

"But you look ill."

She shook her head. "I just need to be alone. Please go! I'll be all right."

Distressed, the girl withdrew. The door closed and Bathsheba crumpled to the ground. Stifling a cry, she stretched out flat on her face, arms outstretched. "Oh, Lord God of Israel, have mercy . . . have mercy upon me." She wept violently.

She had cost the life of yet another of David's sons.

seven

SOLOMON acted quickly to destroy his enemies. Adonijah's execution sent Joab running to the sacred tent of the Lord, where he caught hold of the horns of the altar. King Solomon sent Benaiah out again. "Kill him there beside the altar and bury him. This will remove the guilt of his senseless murders from me and from my father's family. Then the Lord will repay him for the murders of two men who were more righteous and better than he!"

Solomon then deposed Abiathar as priest before the Lord and sent him home to Anathoth to live out his life in disgrace.

The king summoned Shimei and ordered him to remain within the boundaries of Jerusalem. "On the day you cross the Kidron Valley, you will surely die; your blood will be on your own head!" Solomon set guards to watching, knowing it would be only a matter of time before Shimei disobeyed. The day he did, Solomon would execute him for daring to curse God's anointed, King David.

Everyone knew Solomon had his eyes wide open. He'd given notice to all that this king would be watching and holding the reins of the kingdom firmly in his own hands. He would not be manipulated by lesser men.

Bathsheba felt relief rather than joy. Perhaps this bloodshed would now bring peace in Israel. Perhaps the men would no longer need to go out to war against the nations surrounding them. Perhaps there would be a time of plenty in Canaan. Men would toil and enjoy the work of their hands. Surely that would be a great blessing from the Lord.

She'd been born into a time of war. Peace had come infrequently, like a breath of spring in the midst of a long, cold winter, a sweet aroma hinting of what one day would come, but it wouldn't last.

Not in her lifetime.

She was old now, and tired—so very tired. Strange how the past came back so vividly. Poignant memories often gripped her and made her heart ache. Ahithophel, holding her upon his lap, smiling. Her father laughing, his face bronzed by firelight. Her mother holding her close. Uriah dropping the stone she gave him and walking away. And David, always David. He lived in her dreams, agile as a deer leaping to high places, singing songs to his men and leading them out to build a kingdom for God's people. Oh, how she had loved him—and loved him still.

"Mother," came a gentle voice, drawing her back to the present. She blinked and turned her face toward it, smiling.

She brushed Solomon's cheek. The crown rested firmly upon his regal head. He was shrewd and would watch over and protect his brothers. He would seek the Lord's guidance in how to make Israel a beacon to all nations. She need not worry about her sons. Hadn't God put a protective hedge around them from the time they were babies? Hadn't God kept them safe within the walls of a palace torn by intrigue? Whoever would have thought God would put the son of an adulteress on the throne? Who would have imagined *her* son would take the reigns of this unruly nation and make it the center of civilization?

Lord, Your mercy is beyond anything I will ever understand. Far beyond anything I deserve. Help me to give my sons what they need before I go the way of all flesh, back to dust.

"Listen to me, my sons," she said as they gathered around her bed. "Remember your father's instructions, and don't forsake what I've taught you. Fear the Lord, for He holds all power and you will accomplish nothing without Him. Treasure the Lord's commandments more than gold or jewels. Be attentive and incline your heart to understand them. Remember the blessings and the cursings and make wise choices."

She looked at Solomon. He was as handsome as David, but there was a shrewdness about him his father had lacked, an edge of cynicism that made her sad. Perhaps it was the way he had grown up, among power-hungry brothers. She held out her hand and he sat on her couch. Taking her hand, he kissed it.

Shobab, Shimea, and Nathan moved in closer, tears in their eyes.

"You all know how much I loved your father," she said in a trembling voice.

Solomon's hand tightened. "Yes, Mother. No one could doubt your love for David."

"Then please listen with that understanding and save yourselves sorrow."

"She's in pain," Shobab whispered.

"Perhaps we should call her maidservant."

"No," Solomon said, his eyes never leaving hers. "Let her speak."

She sensed there was little time left. "When you marry . . ." She looked around at each of her sons, and then held Solomon's gaze. "Choose a wife carefully from among the maidens of Israel. Find a young woman who fears the Lord, a girl who is trustworthy, who works with her hands and has joy in it, who can manage a household wisely and with compassion, a girl who cares for the poor. Let her be physically strong, so she will be able to give you healthy sons and raise them up to be men after God's own heart. But don't go after a woman simply because she's beautiful." She smiled sadly. "Beauty is often deceitful and vain. You've all grown up with beautiful women around you. You know how treacherous they can be." Hadn't it been her beauty David first lusted after? Hadn't she sensed that with her woman's heart and opened the door for him to sin? Oh, the price they'd both paid for that! She was still paying.

Oh, Lord, let it not be so for my sons. Let them be wise and choose women of virtue, women who love You more than the things of this world, women who love You with all their heart, mind, soul, and might!

She smiled at Solomon. "A woman of virtue will be an excellent wife and a crown for your head. A crown you will look upon with more delight than the one you wear, my son."

She looked at Shobab, Shimea, and Nathan. Fine sons, all of them, each an unexpected blessing from the Lord and evidence of His grace and mercy. *Oh, God, let them hear my instruction.* "A good wife will increase your honor at the gates. She will discipline your sons and raise them up to follow in the ways of the Lord your God. Sons like that will strengthen the house of David and bless our nation."

There was so much more she wanted to say, but she knew better. The longer a mother spoke, the less inclined her sons were to listen. Besides, she had said it all many times before. She had been teaching them from the time they were babies at her breast, boys on her knees, or young men she'd sent away to learn from a prophet of God. *Oh, Lord God of Israel, that You should choose my sons. Your mercy never ceases.* She had done all she could to raise up her sons to love the Lord and serve Him with all their strength. She wanted these young men to be better than their father, David, whom she had loved so much. And still loved. Death could not diminish love.

"I'm very tired." She drank in the sight of each son as he bent down and kissed her, straightened, and walked out the door, returning to his own life and choices.

Solomon lingered. "You were an excellent wife to Abba," he said softly, tears in his eyes. "You didn't honor him in word only, like the others. You honored him in truth and in deed."

"I brought great harm to him."

"And great blessing, too." He smiled. "Four sons, one of whom will be a great king."

"With God's help, my son." She kissed his hand. "Don't ever forget who has the real power."

Her mind drifted. She heard her mother's voice in a distant memory. *"A king must build a strong house and preserve the kingdom."* She gripped his hand tightly. "The life of a king is more difficult than the life of a shepherd, my son. Your father drank from another man's cistern and poisoned his own well." Solomon frowned. His lips parted, but she spoke quickly. "Have you ever loved someone, Solomon, truly loved her?"

"Abishag."

The hair stood on the back of Bathsheba's neck. She thought of David's sending orders to kill Uriah. She remembered Solomon's wrath the day she had gone to ask that the Shunammite be given to Adonijah as a wife.

Solomon leaned down. "No, Mother, I did not order my brother's execution over a woman. I had Adonijah killed because he was intent upon evil. He wanted the throne. Rebellion would've cost thousands of lives and brought chaos to Israel. There is a time for war, Mother. God used King David to subdue the enemies that surround us. It was left to me to destroy the enemies that have dwelt among us. Now, it is time for peace."

Let it be so, Lord; oh, let it be so.

She felt herself growing weaker. "Then keep the well clean," she said softly. "Take Abishag for your wife, for she is everything I've described to you. But remain faithful to her. I know you are a king and can have as many wives and concubines as you want. I know it is the practice of kings, but don't turn your freedom into an opportunity to sin. Rejoice in the wife of your youth."

"I must build my house."

Her heart sank. "No, my son. Let God build your house."

Solomon leaned down and kissed her cheek, and she knew he was a man withdrawing from her woman's counsel. He had entered the courts of men. *Oh, God, will he make the same mistakes his father did? Are men and women all destined to sin? Is it simply their nature to do so? For so it seems. We have the Law, but we can't seem to keep it.*

Solomon rose and stepped back. She stretched out her arm, holding fast to his hand as long as she could. "I love you, Mother," he whispered hoarsely. "I love you, but I must go." She relaxed her hand and his fingers slipped from hers. Her handmaiden opened the door for him and he went out.

Bathsheba sank back against her bed cushions and closed her eyes. *Oh, Lord, only You can save us from ourselves. Come, Lord, come and save us. Come and dwell among us. Walk with us again as You did in the Garden of Eden. Speak with us face-to-face as You did with Moses. Take us up to live with You as You did with Enoch! Change our sinful hearts.*

"My lady," her handmaiden said, her voice tinged with grief.

Bathsheba opened her eyes. "There's nothing to fear." The girl adjusted the covers, briefly covered Bathsheba's hand with her own, and sat again. Bathsheba closed her eyes again and let her mind wander back over the past.

She remembered her mother's angry, embittered words flung in a prophetic curse on her head. *"You've brought shame upon my household! . . . Fool! How many have died because of you? It will all be on your head. . . . People will spit on the ground when you pass by. . . . They will curse the day of your birth! . . . You are cursed among women! Your name will be a byword for adulteress! Your name will be unspoken as long as I live!"*

The pain of rejection stabbed her as fiercely now as it had the day her mother had turned her back and walked out the door. Bathsheba had seen her mother only one time after that—when she lay on her deathbed, too weak to move or speak. Bathsheba had nursed her for several days, praying silently for some way to restore their relationship. But at the last, her mother had turned her face away and died without ever saying a word to her.

And now she lay quiet upon her couch waiting for her own life to end. She hoped it would be soon. She didn't want to live long enough to see her sons fail. And fail they would because they were, after all, only human. What chance had they to live perfect lives before God with David's hot blood running in their veins? David's blood mingled with her own.

"Your name will be unspoken!"

Only the Lord forgets sin. Only God can take it and send it as far away as the East is from the West. Man remembers. Man recounts. Man condemns.

How many years would come and go after she was dust when men and women would still hold up her sins and wave them like a bloody banner? *Will anyone ever see more in me than that one fateful day when David saw me from his roof and called me to his bed?*

She felt warm breath upon her face and a gentle kiss on her forehead.

I see.

Bathsheba's heart raced in joy. She opened her eyes. When had it grown so dark? Her handmaiden slept in the chair beside her bed, but no one else was in the room.

She drew in her breath and smelled incense drifting in the air. It reminded her of the Tent of Meeting; sweet, so sweet, her soul drank it in. She relaxed, her mind drifting again, gently this time, as though floating in a cleansing stream.

I know they will remember my sins, Lord, but when they look upon my life, let them see what You did for an unworthy woman. Let them see the hope born from despair. If they must recount my sins, let them count Your blessings more so. You protected me. You raised me up. You gave me sons. Let my name be unspoken, Lord, for what am I that anyone should remember me? But, oh, Lord God of Israel, if they do remember me, let them open their mouths and sing praises for Your great mercy toward me. Let them see Your infinite grace and Your boundless love. And let them . . .

She sighed deeply.

. . . be encouraged.

DEAR READER,

You have just read the story of Bathsheba as perceived by one author. Is this the whole truth about the story of David and Bathsheba? Jesus said to seek and you will find the answers you need for life. The best way to find the truth is to look for yourself!

This "Seek and Find" section is designed to help you discover the story of Bathsheba as recorded in the Bible. It consists of six short studies that you can do on your own or with a small discussion group.

You may be surprised to learn that this ancient story will have applications for your life today. No matter where we live or in what century, God's Word is truth. It is as relevant today as it was yesterday. In it we find a future and a hope.

Peggy Lynch

the temptation

SEEK GOD'S WORD FOR TRUTH
Read the following passage:

> The following spring, the time of year when kings go to war, David sent Joab and the Israelite army to destroy the Ammonites. In the process they laid siege to the city of Rabbah. But David stayed behind in Jerusalem.
>
> Late one afternoon David got out of bed after taking a nap and went for a stroll on the roof of the palace. As he looked out over the city, he noticed a woman of unusual beauty taking a bath. He sent someone to find out who she was, and he was told, "She is Bathsheba, the daughter of Eliam and the wife of Uriah the Hittite." Then David sent for her; and when she came to the palace, he slept with her. (She had just completed the purification rites after having her menstrual period.) Then she returned home. Later, when Bathsheba discovered that she was pregnant, she sent a message to inform David.   2 SAMUEL 11:1-5

In the spring, kings go off to war. Where was King David this particular spring?

What did David do when he could not sleep?

What did David find out about "the woman" he was watching? List everything he knew *before* he sent for her.

David still had time to change the course of events. However, what course does David take?

From the same verses, list what you learn about "the woman."

From what little is told about the woman, would you describe her
as a seductress, a victim, or something in between? Why?

FIND GOD'S WAYS FOR YOU
Read the following passage:

> Remember, no one who wants to do wrong should ever
> say, "God is tempting me." God is never tempted to do
> wrong, and he never tempts anyone else either. Tempta-
> tion comes from the lure of our own evil desires. These
> evil desires lead to evil actions, and evil actions lead to
> death.   JAMES 1:13-15

Where do temptations come from and where do they lead?

Read the following verse:

> Remember that the temptations that come into your life
> are no different from what others experience. And God is
> faithful. He will keep the temptation from becoming so
> strong that you can't stand up against it. When you are
> tempted, he will show you a way out so that you will not
> give in to it.   1 CORINTHIANS 10:13

What does God say about temptation and what does He offer as a solution?

Look again at 2 Samuel 11:1-5. List the ways of escape you can see that David ignored. Do the same for the woman.

Think about times when you have been tempted. How have you responded and what kind of pattern do you see?

STOP AND PONDER
Look back at 1 Corinthians 10:13. Do you look for ways of escape?

the cover-up

SEEK GOD'S WORD FOR TRUTH
Read the following passage:

So David sent word to Joab: "Send me Uriah the Hittite." When Uriah arrived, David asked him how Joab and the army were getting along and how the war was progressing. Then he told Uriah, "Go on home and relax." David even sent a gift to Uriah after he had left the palace. But Uriah wouldn't go home. He stayed that night at the palace entrance with some of the king's other servants.

When David heard what Uriah had done, he summoned him and asked, "What's the matter with you? Why didn't you go home last night after being away for so long?"

Uriah replied, "The Ark and the armies of Israel and Judah are living in tents, and Joab and his officers are camping in the open fields. How could I go home to wine and dine and sleep with my wife? I swear that I will never be guilty of acting like that."

"Well, stay here tonight," David told him, "and tomorrow you may return to the army." So Uriah stayed in Jerusalem that day and the next. Then David invited him to dinner and got him drunk. But even then he couldn't get Uriah to go home to his wife. Again he slept at the palace entrance.

So the next morning David wrote a letter to Joab and gave it to Uriah to deliver. The letter instructed Joab, "Station Uriah on the front lines where the battle is fiercest. Then pull back so that he will be killed." So Joab assigned Uriah to a spot close to the city wall where he knew the enemy's strongest men were fighting. And Uriah was killed along with several other Israelite soldiers.

The Joab sent a battle report to David. He told his messenger, "Report all the news of the battle to the king. But he might get angry and ask, 'Why did the troops go so close to the city? Didn't they know there would be shooting from the walls? Wasn't Gideon's son Abimelech killed at Thebez by a woman who threw a millstone down on him?' Then tell him, 'Uriah the Hittite was killed, too.' "

So the messenger went to Jerusalem and gave a complete report to David. "The enemy came out against us," he said. "And as we chased them back to the city gates, the archers on the wall shot arrows at us. Some of our men were killed, including Uriah the Hittite."

"Well, tell Joab not to be discouraged," David said. "The sword kills one as well as another! Fight harder next time, and conquer the city!"

When Bathsheba heard that her husband was dead, she mourned for him. When the period of mourning was over, David sent for her and brought her to the palace, and she became one of his wives. Then she gave birth to a son. But the Lord was very displeased with what David had done.

2 SAMUEL 11:6-27

Bathsheba sent a message to the king informing him she was pregnant. How did King David respond? What instructions did he give Uriah?

What was the motivation for Uriah's actions?

David writes a letter to Joab. In your own words, describe David's new plan and his attitude.

How did Bathsheba react to her husband's death? What do you gather from her reaction?

What happened to Bathsheba after her time of mourning was over?

Contrast the actions and attitudes of David, Uriah, and Bathsheba.

FIND GOD'S WAYS FOR YOU
Bathsheba chose to rely on David to take care of "the problem."
David chose to handle things himself. And Uriah became the
scapegoat.

When you make wrong choices, what kind of pattern do you fall
into?

How have you helped cover up for other people?

What impact have your choices had on others?

What impact have other people's choices had on your life?

STOP AND PONDER
There is a path before each person that seems right, but it ends
in death.   PROVERBS 14:12

Where are you headed?

the confession

Read the following passage:

So the Lord sent Nathan the prophet to tell David this story: "There were two men in a certain town. One was rich, and one was poor. The rich man owned many sheep and cattle. The poor man owned nothing but a little lamb he had worked hard to buy. He raised that little lamb, and it grew up with his children. It ate from the man's own plate and drank from his cup. He cuddled it in his arms like a baby daughter. One day a guest arrived at the home of the rich man. But instead of killing a lamb from his own flocks for food, he took the poor man's lamb and killed it and served it to his guest."

David was furious. "As surely as the Lord lives," he vowed, "any man who would do such a thing deserves to die! He must repay four lambs to the poor man for the one he stole and for having no pity."

Then Nathan said to David, "You are that man! The Lord, the God of Israel, says, 'I anointed you king of Israel and saved you from the power of Saul. I gave you his house and his wives and the kingdoms of Israel and Judah. And if that had not been enough, I would have given you much, much more. Why, then, have you despised the word of the Lord and done this horrible deed? For you have murdered Uriah and stolen his wife. From this time on, the sword will be a constant threat to your family, because you have despised me by taking Uriah's wife to be your own.

"'Because of what you have done, I, the Lord, will cause your own household to rebel against you. I will give your wives to another man, and he will go to bed with them in public view. You did it secretly, but I will do this to you openly in the sight of all Israel.'"

Then David confessed to Nathan, "I have sinned against the Lord."   2 SAMUEL 12:1-13A

How does the Lord confront David?

How does David view the man in the story?

Why do you think Nathan had to bluntly tell David, "You are that man!"?

As God lays bare the extent of David's sin, what does He say will happen to David's house and why?

What further consequences will befall David's family?

What is David's confession?

FIND GOD'S WAYS FOR YOU

Remember a time when someone confronted you about your actions or words or choices. How did you respond or react, and why?

How quickly do you recognize sin in your life?

What kind of consequences are you living with because of your own wrong choices or the wrong choices of someone close to you?

When you face your own sin, do you hide it, handle it, or confess it?

STOP AND PONDER

> Search me, O God, and know my heart; test me and know
> my thoughts. Point out anything in me that offends you,
> and lead me along the path of everlasting life.

PSALM 139:23-24

What do you need to confess to God right now?

forgiveness

SEEK GOD'S WORD FOR TRUTH
Read the following passage:

> Then David confessed to Nathan, "I have sinned against
> the Lord."
>
> Nathan replied, "Yes, but the Lord has forgiven you,
> and you won't die for this sin. But you have given the
> enemies of the Lord great opportunity to despise and blas-
> pheme him, so your child will die."
>
> After Nathan returned to his home, the Lord made
> Bathsheba's baby deathly ill. David begged God to spare
> the child. He went without food and lay all night on the
> bare ground. The leaders of the nation pleaded with him
> to get up and eat with them, but he refused. Then on the
> seventh day the baby died. David's advisers were afraid
> to tell him. "He was so broken up about the baby being
> sick," they said. "What will he do to himself when we tell
> him the child is dead?"

But when David saw them whispering, he realized what had happened. "Is the baby dead?" he asked.

"Yes," they replied. Then David got up from the ground, washed himself, put on lotions, and changed his clothes. Then he went to the Tabernacle and worshiped the Lord. After that, he returned to the palace and ate. His advisers were amazed. "We don't understand you," they told him. "While the baby was still living, you wept and refused to eat. But now that the baby is dead, you have stopped your mourning and are eating again."

David replied, "I fasted and wept while the child was alive, for I said, 'Perhaps the Lord will be gracious to me and let the child live.' But why should I fast when he is dead? Can I bring him back again? I will go to him one day, but he cannot return to me."   2 SAMUEL 12:13-23

What does God do with David's sin? And what is the good news about David's life?

What shocking news does Nathan give David?

What does David do and for how long?

How does David react when the child dies?

Where does he go and what extraordinary thing does he do?

David's advisers were baffled by his actions. What comfort and hope motivated David?

FIND GOD'S WAYS FOR YOU
Read the following verse:

> If we confess our sins to him, he is faithful and just to
> forgive us and to cleanse us from every wrong.
>
> 1 JOHN 1:9

From this Scripture, what is God's promise? What is the condition
of that promise?

Have you experienced forgiveness? How do you know you've been
forgiven? How willing are you to forgive others?

Read the following passage:

> The Lord is merciful and gracious; he is slow to get angry
> and full of unfailing love. He will not constantly accuse
> us, nor remain angry forever. He has not punished us for
> all our sins, nor does he deal with us as we deserve. For his
> unfailing love toward those who fear him is as great as the
> height of the heavens above the earth. He has removed our
> rebellious acts as far away from us as the east is from the
> west. The Lord is like a father to his children, tender and
> compassionate to those who fear him. For he understands
> how weak we are; he knows we are only dust. PSALM 103:8-14

List everything you learn in this Scripture about how God deals with you and sin.

STOP AND PONDER
Read the following passage:

> So now there is no condemnation for those who belong to Christ Jesus. For the power of the life-giving Spirit has freed you through Christ Jesus from the power of sin that leads to death.
> ROMANS 8:1-2

Who owns you?

SEEK GOD'S WORD FOR TRUTH

Read the following passage:

> Then David comforted Bathsheba, his wife, and slept with
> her. She became pregnant and gave birth to a son, and
> they named him Solomon. The Lord loved the child and
> sent word through Nathan the prophet that his name
> should be Jedidiah—"beloved of the Lord"—because the
> Lord loved him.   2 SAMUEL 12:24-25

David confessed to God. David waited on God. David worshiped God.
David believed God for the future. These steps lead to a restored relationship with God. What does David now do concerning Bathsheba?

What did God do for Bathsheba?

Who named the baby Solomon?

What message did God send to Bathsheba through Nathan the prophet?

God sent Nathan to confront David regarding his sin. What was the purpose of Nathan's visit to Bathsheba?

From the above passage, what evidence do you find that Bathsheba also experienced a restored relationship with God?

FIND GOD'S WAYS FOR YOU
What does *restoration* mean to you?

Read the following passage:

> Dear brothers and sisters, if another Christian is over-
> come by some sin, you who are godly should gently and
> humbly help that person back onto the right path. And be
> careful not to fall into the same temptation yourself. Share
> each other's troubles and problems, and in this way obey
> the law of Christ.   GALATIANS 6:1-2

What role do we have in helping one another be restored to God?

What attitude are you to have when others need to be restored?

Are you seeking restoration? What steps do you need to take?

STOP AND PONDER

> God saved you by his special favor when you believed.
> And you can't take credit for this; it is a gift from God.
> Salvation is not a reward for the good things we have
> done, so none of us can boast about it. For we are God's
> masterpiece. He has created us anew in Christ Jesus, so
> that we can do the good things he planned for us long ago.
>
> EPHESIANS 2:8-10

Are you a new creation?

blessings

SEEK GOD'S WORD FOR TRUTH

Traditionally, Bathsheba is remembered for her adulterous affair with King David and is referred to as "the wife of Uriah." But let's recount how God remembers her. Read the following passages:

> Then David moved the capital to Jerusalem, where he reigned another thirty-three years. The sons born to David in Jerusalem included Shimea, Shobab, Nathan, and Solomon. Bathsheba, the daughter of Ammiel [Eliam], was the mother of these sons.   1 CHRONICLES 3:4B-5

What did God do for Bathsheba?

Then Nathan the prophet went to Bathsheba, Solomon's mother, and asked her, "Did you realize that Haggith's son, Adonijah, has made himself king and that our lord David doesn't even know about it? If you want to save your own life and the life of your son Solomon, follow my counsel. Go at once to King David and say to him, 'My lord, didn't you promise me that my son Solomon would be the next king and would sit upon your throne? Then why has Adonijah become king?' And while you are still talking with him, I will come and confirm everything you have said."   1 KINGS 1:11-14

List everything that shows God's continued care for Bathsheba.

"Call Bathsheba," David said. So she came back in and stood before the king. And the king vowed, "As surely as the Lord lives, who has rescued me from every danger, today I decree that your son Solomon will be the next king and will sit on my throne, just as I swore to you before the Lord, the God of Israel."

Then Bathsheba bowed low before him again and exclaimed, "May my lord King David live forever!"
                                                          1 KINGS 1:28-31

How did David continue to support and comfort Bathsheba?

All the royal officials went to King David and congratulated him, saying, "May your God make Solomon's fame even greater than your own, and may Solomon's kingdom be even greater than yours!" Then the king bowed his head in worship as he lay in his bed, and he spoke these words: "Blessed be the Lord, the God of Israel, who today has chosen someone to sit on my throne while I am still alive to see it."   1 KINGS 1:47-48

How did God keep His promise to Bathsheba? What was David's response?

Young Woman: "Go out to look upon King Solomon, O young women of Jerusalem. See the crown with which his mother crowned him on his wedding day, the day of his gladness."   SONG OF SONGS 3:11

What further joy did Bathsheba have?

Jesse was the father of King David. David was the father of
Solomon (his mother was Bathsheba, the widow of Uriah).
Jacob was the father of Joseph, the husband of Mary.
Mary was the mother of Jesus, who is called the Messiah.

MATTHEW 1:6, 16

What ultimate blessing was bestowed upon Bathsheba?

FIND GOD'S WAYS FOR YOU
How do you think you'll be remembered?

How would you like to be remembered?

How has God blessed you?

Trace God's hand of mercy in your life.

STOP AND PONDER

> "For I know the plans I have for you," says the Lord.
> "They are plans for good and not for disaster, to give you
> a future and a hope. In those days when you pray, I will
> listen. If you look for me in earnest, you will find me
> when you seek me. I will be found by you," says the Lord.
>
> JEREMIAH 29:11-14A

Jesus has found you. Have you found Him? He's waiting.

the genealogy of JESUS the CHRIST

THIS is a record of the ancestors of Jesus the Messiah, a descendant of King David and of Abraham:

Abraham was the father of Isaac.
Isaac was the father of Jacob.
Jacob was the father of Judah and his brothers.
Judah was the father of Perez and Zerah (their mother was **Tamar**).
Perez was the father of Hezron.
Hezron was the father of Ram.
Ram was the father of Amminadab.
Amminadab was the father of Nahshon.
Nahshon was the father of Salmon.
Salmon was the father of Boaz (his mother was **Rahab**).
Boaz was the father of Obed (his mother was **Ruth**).
Obed was the father of Jesse.
Jesse was the father of King David.
David was the father of Solomon (his mother was **Bathsheba,** the widow of Uriah).

Solomon was the father of Rehoboam.
Rehoboam was the father of Abijah.
Abijah was the father of Asaph.
Asaph was the father of Jehoshaphat.
Jehoshaphat was the father of Jehoram.
Jehoram was the father of Uzziah.
Uzziah was the father of Jotham.
Jotham was the father of Ahaz.
Ahaz was the father of Hezekiah.
Hezekiah was the father of Manasseh.
Manasseh was the father of Amos.
Amos was the father of Josiah.
Josiah was the father of Jehoiachin and his brothers (born at the time of the exile to Babylon).
After the Babylonian exile:
Jehoiachin was the father of Shealtiel.
Shealtiel was the father of Zerubbabel.
Zerubbabel was the father of Abiud.
Abiud was the father of Eliakim.
Eliakim was the father of Azor.
Azor was the father of Zadok.
Zadok was the father of Akim.
Akim was the father of Eliud.
Eliud was the father of Eleazar.
Eleazar was the father of Matthan.
Matthan was the father of Jacob.
Jacob was the father of Joseph, the husband of Mary.
Mary was the mother of Jesus, who is called the Messiah.

MATTHEW 1:1-16

about the author

FRANCINE RIVERS has been writing for more than twenty years. From 1976 to 1985 she had a successful writing career in the general market and won numerous awards. After becoming a born-again Christian in 1986, Francine wrote *Redeeming Love* as her statement of faith.

Since then, Francine has published numerous books in the CBA market and has continued to win both industry acclaim and reader loyalty. Her novel *The Last Sin Eater* won the ECPA Gold Medallion, and three of her books have won the prestigious Romance Writers of America Rita Award.

Francine says she uses her writing to draw closer to the Lord, that through her work she might worship and praise Jesus for all he has done and is doing in her life.

books by francine rivers

The Mark of the Lion trilogy
A Voice in the Wind
An Echo in the Darkness
As Sure As the Dawn

The Scarlet Thread   *The Last Sin Eater*
The Atonement Child   *Leota's Garden*
Redeeming Love   *The Shoe Box*

A Lineage of Grace series
Unveiled   *Unspoken*
Unashamed   *Unafraid*
Unshaken